Who Killed Coriolanus?

A Novel By

Ron Fritsch

ISBN: 979-8985072617

Published by Asymmetric Worlds

For information, address:

ronfritsch@ronfritsch.com

Front cover art: *Self-portrait as Paris* by Anthony van Dyck (circa 1628)

For David, Lee Ann and my family

The Characters

Characters living during the time of this novel:

Note: Sparta was one of several Greek kingdoms.

Brutus, the leader of the Roman plebeians

Coriolanus (also known as Old Marco), the commander of the Roman army and navy, Marco's father

Domenic, Old Marco's servant, Philo's companion

Helen, the queen of Sparta, Timon and Hermione's mother, Menelaus's wife, Paris's wife during the Trojan war, Leda's daughter

Hermione, the princess of Sparta, Timon's half-sister, Helen and Menelaus's daughter, Leda's granddaughter

Leda, Helen's mother, Timon and Hermione's grandmother

Livia, a high-ranking warrior in the Roman army

Lukas, Timon's companion

Marco, Old Marco's son

Menelaus, the king of Sparta, Helen's husband, Timon's stepfather, Hermione's father

Old Marco (also known as Coriolanus), the commander of the Roman army and navy, Marco's father

Orestes, a Greek king, Clytemnestra and Agamemnon's son

Philo, Old Marco's servant, Domenic's companion

Thalia, a Spartan trader and ship captain

Timon, Lukas's companion, Helen's son, Paris's son, Menelaus's stepson, Hermione's half-brother, Leda's grandson

Characters mentioned but no longer living during the time of this novel:

Achilles, a Greek king during the Trojan War

Agamemnon, a Greek king during the Trojan War, Clytemnestra's husband, Menelaus's brother, Orestes's father, Atreus's son

Atreus, a former king of Sparta, Menelaus and Agamemnon's father

Clytemnestra, a Greek queen during the Trojan war, Agamemnon's wife, Orestes's mother, Helen's sister

Hector, a prince of Troy during the Trojan War, Paris's brother, Timon's uncle, Hecuba and Priam's son

Hecuba, the queen of Troy during the Trojan War, Priam's wife, Paris and Hector's mother, Timon's grandmother

Paris, a prince of Troy, Helen's husband during the Trojan War, Timon's father, Hector's brother, Hecuba and Priam's son

Priam, the king of Troy during the Trojan War, Hecuba's husband, Paris and Hector's father, Timon's grandfather

Chapter One

Timon

Until the summer day before the day I turned eighteen and became an adult, I had no idea who I was. I only knew my name and my birthdate. Then Helen, who'd married Menelaus and become the queen of Sparta after the Trojan War, told me she was my mother. Paris, the Trojan prince she'd sailed to Troy with before the war, was my father.

I was their legitimate son. They'd married ten months before I was born. After the Trojan War and the deaths of my father, my childless uncle Hector and my paternal grandparents Priam and Hecuba, who'd been the king and queen of Troy, I was the sole surviving member of the Trojan royal family.

My mother and Menelaus brought me to Greece after the war. I was one year old. They couldn't disclose my identity to the people, who would've killed me as soon as they found out who my father was. So I grew to adulthood in the Spartan orphanage. Menelaus, my stepfather, had placed it under my mother's supervision.

I'm certain she would've insisted the orphanage guardians treat the children in their care humanely even if I hadn't been one of them. She'd grown to adulthood in the same orphanage but with guardians who forced the children to earn their upkeep by doing work adults would've found arduous. The cruelty caused the deaths of more than half the orphans before they became adults. Their early deaths decreased the expenses of the institution even more than their continued work would've increased its income.

Menelaus's father Atreus and his older brother Agamemnon ruled Sparta in those days. Menelaus told me himself they had no more sympathy for the common people than a hungry wolf has for its prey.

Because I learned who I was seventeen years after the end of the war, I chose to reveal to the Greek people my identity as well as the true story of how I'd come to dwell in Sparta. From that day forward, I lived in the palace with my mother and stepfather as well as my maternal grandmother Leda, my half-sister Hermione and my companion from the orphanage, Lukas. Nobody attempted to kill or harm me. My continued existence proved the Greek people had gotten over a war they'd supposedly won but knew damned well their victory was meaningless.

Early in the following spring, Lukas and I, who were still eighteen, learned Marco, the son of the commander of the army and navy of Rome, was on his way to see us. Nobody could tell us, though, what the purpose of his visit was.

Marco

The Trojans who survived the Greek siege, invasion and destruction of Troy made their way to Italy. My father and I were among them. I was one year old then. Our people built a city we called Rome.

We knew Paris and Helen had married during the war and she'd given birth to their son. Until recently, though, we hadn't known whether he'd survived the war. If he had, where was he?

Then we learned, from the people who traded goods with the Greeks, he was living with his mother Helen, now the queen of Sparta, and her second husband Menelaus, the king of Sparta.

We hadn't previously heard about Timon because Helen and Menelaus had concealed his existence until he turned eighteen and became an adult. They'd feared their fellow Greeks, who'd suffered the loss of so many loved ones and so much treasure during the war, wouldn't hesitate to kill a son of the Trojan prince who'd sailed to Troy with Helen in the abduction or elopement precipitating the conflict.

The Greeks had another reason to despise Paris and want to terminate the existence of his son. They'd never imagined a Trojan archer could be so lethal. Firing down from the watchtowers and rooftops of Troy, he'd killed far more Greeks than any other Trojan warrior had.

The Romans admired his older brother Hector and considered

him a hero of the war. He'd fought a lengthy duel with Achilles and fell victim to the Greek hero's spear only after a stumble as slight and momentary as the disturbance of the breeze in the wake of the flight of a sparrow.

The Romans, though, loved the memory of Paris even more. To fire the arrow piercing the heart of Achilles, he'd exposed himself to a Greek archer he knew was at least as skillful as he was. He took her arrow deep in his gut and bled to death in Helen's arms.

After Rome heard the news from Greece concerning Timon, my father put me on a Greek merchant ship bound for Sparta. Thalia, the trader who owned and captained the ship, had promised my father she'd introduce me to Helen, Menelaus and Timon.

Like Timon and Lukas, his companion who'd grown up with him in the orphanage, I was eighteen.

Timon

After my mother told me who I was, Lukas and I moved into a chamber in the Spartan palace and began earning our keep in the royal olive grove. We'd learned what to do in the smaller grove we'd managed during our last year in the orphanage. We were pleased the profit we made from the sale of the royal table olives, olive oil and olivewood helped to support the Spartans who couldn't support themselves.

While we worked, Lukas and I composed the songs we sang in the great hall in the palace for anybody who wished to hear us. We rarely gave a performance with a place to sit or stand not taken. We assumed my sudden celebrity as the son of Helen and Paris had more to do with the attendance at our concerts than our talent did. Many people, though, were kind enough to tell us they disagreed with that view.

Thalia, the ship-owning trader who acted as Menelaus and Helen's emissary to Rome, brought Marco to the palace. My mother and Menelaus gave him the directions for the walk he needed to take to the olive grove. Lukas and I and the other workers were busy with the springtime pruning of our trees.

We spotted Marco coming down the path from the palace to the grove. He was as tall and powerfully built as Thalia had described him to us.

"He's not too big for me," Lukas said. "I'll fight him, if that's what he wants."

I laughed. "I doubt he's traveled so far just to pick a fight."

"You never know."

Despite talking as if he were still living in the orphanage and hadn't yet reached his tenth birthday—for our amusement, I assumed—Lukas couldn't take his eyes off our guest.

Marco had umber eyes and hair and a mouth that seemed to be asking for a kiss. He and Lukas and I could've been brothers. Thalia had told us Marco followed the Roman custom and would be as clean-shaven as we and other Greek men were. He was.

When he came within earshot, I spoke to him. "I'm Timon. The man next to me ogling you is Lukas. I assume you're Marco."

Thalia hadn't neglected to inform us Marco, like most Romans, could speak Greek fluently.

He smiled as if he were a tourist who'd reached his destination and liked what he saw.

"I'm Marco," he said. "I doubt a Roman exists who wouldn't envy me for being in your presence."

The expression on Marco's face told me I must've given away my lack of preparation for that remark.

He'd come as close to Lukas and me as we were to each other.

"Your mother and father," he said, "were Helen and Paris. She helped feed the people in Troy during the war. Priam and Hecuba had placed her in charge of all the orchards, gardens, vineyards and groves within the walls of the city. She held a shield for your father on the rooftops. He took positions on them to shoot at the invaders with his arrows. Some of the older Romans say they saw your mother behind her own shield feeding you from her breasts."

10

Who Killed Coriolanus?

I hadn't heard about feeding from my mother's breasts behind her shield before, but I didn't doubt the story was true. I was a suckling child when my father fired arrows at the invading Greeks from the rooftops in Troy.

"Then we learned," Marco continued, "you were alive. You'd spent your childhood not knowing who you were. Your mother had placed you in an orphanage she oversaw. She made certain the guardians treated all the orphans humanely. What a story that was to our ears."

I could see, out of the corner of my eye, Lukas was as surprised by our guest's comments as I was.

Marco turned to Lukas. "I know who you are. You grew up with Timon in the orphanage. You became companions there. You sing together. You compose your own songs. People flock to your performances. That's another story I enjoyed hearing."

Lukas seldom took a pass on an opportunity to pry. Nor did he then.

"Do you have a companion?" he asked our guest.

Marco shook his head. "Not yet. If I had one, he'd be with me."

Marco

Timon and Lukas were as pleasing to my eyes as Thalia had told me they'd be. She said they were the hardest-working managers of an olive grove she'd come across in her travels. As soon as I saw them, I envied them.

After I'd turned eighteen and become a warrior, I spent some time in my bed with one of my security guards, who was also eighteen. My father encouraged that sort of thing among his warriors and sailors, and in whatever form it took. So long, he said, as both, or all, the persons involved in it consented to it.

The warrior I liked, though, wasn't ready for a companion. He was looking for the person he thought would please him the most at the moment. Sometimes I was that person. Sometimes I wasn't. A number

11

of other warriors appeared to please him, at any given time at least, as much as I did. Companionship, he instructed me, came later, like autumn leaves, winter, old age and death.

But what I was looking for is what Timon and Lukas had.

Timon

Marco threw an arm around Lukas's shoulders.

Lukas welcomed the familiarity. I'd already guessed he would.

"Thalia told me," Marco said, "you lost your parents in the war."

"I did," Lukas said. "I was only two months old when they died. They were digging the tunnel that ended up inside the walls of Troy. It collapsed on them. They hadn't chosen to be there. Agamemnon's warriors forced them, and other young people like them, to assist the Greek armies in their glorious siege and destruction of Troy."

Marco shook his head. "Only two months old?"

"I never knew either of them," Lukas said. "They were shepherds tending sheep and goats in the hills of Sparta before the war."

"I was only a year old," Marco said, "when I lost my mother."

"How did that happen?" I asked.

"My parents and I were fleeing Troy in a carriage. A Greek archer in a chariot caught up with us. My mother cradled me in her arms to make sure I wouldn't get shot. The archer got off one arrow. It struck my mother between her shoulders. When my father reached safety and was able to bring the horses to a halt, he saw I was on the floor of the carriage covered with my mother's blood. My mother was dead."

Lukas grimaced. "That was the monster Agamemnon's doing. He didn't want anybody escaping Troy."

I turned to Marco. "I'm sorry your mother died, but I'm damned glad the monster didn't succeed in killing every Trojan. Neither you nor I would be here now talking about it."

Chapter Two

Marco

On our way back to the palace, I walked with Timon and Lukas through the olive grove they managed. I told them I lived on my father's estate south of the city of Rome. We had olive groves, orchards, vineyards, gardens, wheat and barley fields, and pastures and barns for our cattle, sheep and goats.

When Timon and Lukas questioned me about them, they could tell I knew next to nothing about such matters. I told them the truth. My father had always insisted I'd waste my time learning how to grow plants and raise animals. He employed plebeians who knew very well how to do those things. His only child needed to be a warrior, like him.

I discovered my hosts and I were, in that sense, direct opposites. They assured me they'd never had any interest in becoming warriors.

"My father," I said, seeking to change the subject, "sent me here to accomplish one thing."

"What would that be?" Lukas asked.

I'd rehearsed my reply to the question endlessly. "I'm here to extend to both of you personally my father's heartfelt invitation to Rome. He says he'll make your visit to our city as pleasant as the son of Paris and Helen, and his companion, deserve."

As soon as those words were out of my mouth, Timon's facial expression told me I'd most likely go home to my father empty-handed.

"I understand," Timon said, "the Romans have given your father a new name."

I hadn't anticipated that response to my father's invitation.

"That's right," I said. "His original name was Marco, but after I was born, everybody called him Old Marco to distinguish him from me. They never called me Young Marco, though. I've always simply been Marco. Now my father's legal name is Coriolanus."

Ron Fritsch

Timon

During an evening meal at the palace prior to Marco's arrival, Thalia, our guest, had explained how the commander of the Roman army and navy had acquired his new name.

Rome and the neighboring Volscian kingdom had disputed, for many years, which of them had the right to rule a city lying on their border.

"By the way," Thalia said, "Rome isn't a kingdom."

"What is it?" Lukas asked.

"It's a republic," she replied. "A consul, elected by its senate, rules it, with the advice and consent of the senate. The people elect the senators."

During the previous autumn, Thalia told us, Old Marco chose to end the dispute between the Romans and the Volscians once and for all. He refused to wait for the Roman consul and senate to decide what to do. He led an invasion of the disputed city by the Roman navy and army. His forces destroyed the fleet defending the city in its harbor, broke through its gates and captured it.

"The name of the city is Coriolis," Thalia said. "The warriors in Old Marco's army and the sailors in his navy demanded the Romans demonstrate their gratitude to him by giving him a new name to honor his victory, Coriolanus. The senate and consul went along with the army and navy's request and legally changed his name."

My mother couldn't conceal her disgust. "This victorious general sounds too much like Agamemnon to me."

My stepfather Menelaus, my maternal grandmother Leda, and my half-sister Hermione nodded their agreement.

I turned to Thalia. "Do all the Roman people elect the senators?"

"That question," Thalia replied, "came up toward the end of last summer."

Romans, she told us, were either patricians or plebeians. The patricians owned land or substantial property, like a ship or a place to sell

14

goods in a market. The far more numerous plebeians were the workers who either paid rent for their dwellings or lived in quarters their employers provided for them. Until last summer, only the patricians had the right to vote for senators.

"Brutus," Thalia said, "changed that."

"Who's Brutus?" Lukas asked.

"The patricians," Thalia said, "call him the self-appointed spokesperson for the plebeians."

Last summer he'd led them in rioting over the prices the patricians charged for their grain, which were the prices the senate determined. He brought to the Curia, the building where the senators met and the consul held court, the bodies of children and elderly people he claimed had died of hunger because their families couldn't afford to buy the grain to bake the bread that would've kept them alive.

The senate, Brutus charged, would rather see children and their grandparents dead than require the patricians to sell grain to the working people at prices they could pay.

Thalia went on to tell us Brutus stopped the rioting only after the patricians gave the plebeians the right to vote in the next and subsequent elections.

"But the next election hasn't been held yet," she said. "So the patricians still control the senate, the consulship and the grain prices. When the next election is held, everybody assumes Brutus will run for the consulship himself."

Marco

On our way to the palace, Lukas and Timon and I stopped to see the swans Helen's mother Leda cared for. We sat on a bench overlooking their pond. I liked how close Timon and Lukas were on either side of me. I'd have to admit, though, I'd chosen the bench, and it was no doubt intended to seat only two people.

"Your father and you," Lukas said to me, "are patricians."

I nodded. "We're patricians."

"We don't have patricians and plebeians in Greece," Lukas said.

I nodded again. "My tutors told me that."

Timon looked at me. "You and your father fled Troy. How did he become the owner of an estate in Rome?"

"It's no secret," I said. "His family owned a considerable amount of farmland outside the walls of Troy. After the Greek kings threatened to besiege the city, my father's family contributed everything they owned except their land to the people inside the city walls—their herds of livestock, and all the grain, beans, lentils and other crops they had in their barns. My father took his family's gold and silver with him when he fled to Italy. He therefore had the right and the means to buy any land he chose. As a result, he owns one of the largest and most productive estates in the Roman republic. He also knew what he was doing. He hired the most capable people to run it for him."

"And those people," Lukas asked, "are plebeians?"

"They're plebeians," I said. "They don't own property. Their children have no obligation to train to become warriors."

"Did any of your father's workers," Timon asked, "participate in the protests or riots Brutus organized?"

I hadn't imagined my hosts in Sparta would ask me such questions. My father had given me no warning they would.

I shook my head.

"Did they fear," Lukas asked, "your father would've asked them to leave his estate if they'd supported Brutus publicly?"

I shrugged. "I doubt he would've done that. He values them all."

"Do you think," Timon asked, "any of them supported Brutus privately?"

I shrugged again. "I can imagine some of them might've. They've always maintained friendly relations with me, though. I can't complain they've ever been unkind to me."

Timon

16

Who Killed Coriolanus?

My mother and Menelaus insisted Lukas and I didn't need to help prepare the meal that evening. They said we and Marco should take our seats at the table in the dining room and get started on the wine.

"I never thought," Marco said, "the members of a royal family would prepare their own meals. Don't they employ servants to do that?"

"Absolutely not," Lukas said. "This isn't an ordinary royal family. This one has to be feeding twenty or more guests before they'll consider hiring people to prepare the food—unless, of course, it's an occasion when the guests bring food of their own to share."

Marco blinked his eyes.

"They told me," Lukas said, "they're roasting duck this evening. That's why we're drinking white wine. I can get you some red, though, if you'd prefer it."

Marco shook his head. "Your white wine is perfect. I look forward to the duck."

Marco

The absence of servants wasn't the only surprise for me during the first meal I ate with the Spartan royal family. Their seating arrangement was unusual too.

They sat at one end of a table that looked as if it could accommodate three or four times as many people. But the king didn't sit at the head of it. Leda sat there. Her granddaughter Hermione, who was sixteen, sat in the first chair on her left, followed by Helen and Menelaus. Leda's grandson Timon occupied the first position on her right. Ordinarily, they told me, Lukas would sit in the chair to the right of Timon's, but as long as I was a guest in the palace, that was where I was to sit, directly across the table from Helen, and with Lukas next to me on my right.

Because they had nobody to serve the food, all of us, including the king and queen, picked up plates and bowls from stacks at the end of a counter in the kitchen and proceeded down the length of it, where containers, positioned next to serving forks and ladles, held various items of food. We forked onto our plates and ladled into our bowls whatever we chose, carried our food to the dining room table, sat down and began eating immediately—"while it's still hot," they said—without bothering to wait for the others to sit down with their plates and bowls.

I wondered if this was the way plebeian families dined in Rome. It seemed to me a reasonable way to handle matters if one had no employees to do the work.

Timon

I knew Lukas would let the others know what he thought they needed to know as soon as they were all seated.

"Marco's father," he said, "has invited Timon and me to Rome. We're to travel there on Thalia's ship when Marco returns to Italy."

My mother, stepfather, sister and grandmother looked up from their food and stared at Marco. I'd assumed the invitation would catch their attention.

Chapter Three

Timon

My mother turned to me. "Do you wish to pay a visit to Rome?"

"I can't imagine," I said, "why I'd wish to do that. The Romans have chosen a republican form of government. I'm the sole surviving member of their former royal family. I can't help but think they'd consider my presence in their country an intrusion, if not a provocation."

I could see, out of the corner of my eye, Marco shaking his head like a dog coming out of the water after a swim.

"No," he said, "that isn't the way the Romans will view you. They'll be pleased to see, at long last, the son and only child of two of the people they admire the most—the two people who could've saved Troy if Hector had given them the chance."

"They don't think," Leda asked, "Paris and Helen started a senseless and horrific war by running off to Troy together?"

Marco shook his head again. "They never thought that. They used to assume Helen and Paris had eloped to Troy, but they never believed that was a sufficient excuse for the Greek kingdoms to besiege, invade and destroy a beautiful city. And now every last Roman has heard the true story, the story Thalia brought to tell us as soon as she'd heard it here in Greece. Nobody has the slightest doubt about any part of it. Agamemnon forced his brother, his brother's bride-to-be and Paris to do what they did. Then, during the terrible war Agamemnon brought down upon both the Trojans and the Greeks, Paris discovered he was digging a tunnel under the walls of Troy. Helen believed him, but Hector stubbornly and tragically wouldn't let them tell the Trojans they were in great danger. The Romans would love to see the grown son of those two people."

I hadn't anticipated Marco would be such a forceful speaker.

"Nobody could deny," I said, "the two people you speak of were exceptionally heroic. My father risked his life to pierce the heart of Achilles, no less, with his arrow. My mother remarkably survived the war, returned home and became the queen of the most enlightened and benevolent kingdom in the world."

"Yes!" Leda said, raising her cup of wine.

"Yes!" Hermione agreed, touching her cup of wine against her grandmother's.

"Yes!" Menelaus, Lukas and I said, also raising our cups of wine.

"But I don't see," I said, "how their accomplishments confer any special status on me just because I turned out to be their son."

Under the table Marco's bare knee gently touched my bare thigh.

I turned to him. "My companion and I are happy in Sparta picking olives and pressing them for their oil. Aren't the people who pick and press olives in Rome considered plebeians?"

Leda chose to speak next, without waiting to hear the answer to my question. "You and Lukas also make the larks jealous with your music."

Hemione nodded. "You and Lukas also compose your own music. My tutor tells me you're the first musicians in at least a century who've done that."

Marco turned to me. He'd seen fit to leave his knee against my thigh. "When do I get to hear you and Lukas play your instruments and sing your songs?"

"That comes later," Lukas replied. "After we've finished our meal and washed and dried the dishes."

I hadn't taken my eyes off Marco. "You can be glad you're our guest. You won't have to help us with the dishes."

"I'll do it anyway," he said.

Hermione, who was first in the line of succession to the throne of Sparta, laughed. "You'll be the only warrior I can remember helping us in the kitchen."

She'd remarked earlier to Lukas and me on our guest's sizable biceps and muscular body.

Leda turned to Marco. "When my beautiful swans saw you this afternoon, were they jealous?"

"They were," Lukas said. "I could see how upset they were. But I couldn't blame them. I felt for them as if I were one of them."

Marco laughed. "They seemed perfectly unbothered to me."

I laughed. "Lukas wasn't unbothered."

Timon

Lukas and I said good night to Marco at the door to the chamber he'd occupy while he was our guest. Then we went to see my mother and Menelaus in her chamber, as they'd requested.

"I can understand," my mother said, "the people of Rome would like to see the son of Paris. His parents and his brother Hector never gave him any role to play in governing Troy, not even when the Greek armies came for me. But the people truly loved him. They told me, more than a few times, he was one of them. I could see it too. Priam, Hecuba and Hector—especially Hector—kept the people at arm's length. Paris used any excuse he could to throw his arms around people."

Menelaus laughed. "He even did that with me. And I was supposedly his rival for Helen."

"But the people of Rome," I said, "haven't invited me to their city. The man now known as Coriolanus has. And he's a patrician—a high-ranking patrician too."

"But don't you think," Menelaus asked, "if the Romans saw you in person, they'd understand you're just as much a working person as most of them are?"

"I'd hope so," I replied. "But they might also believe I'm the sole surviving member of their former royal family making an attempt to appear to be one of them."

Lukas found my argument amusing. "You've never seemed very

royal to me. I was the most surprised person in the world when I found out you, a worker, were the son of Helen and Paris. I doubt you'd have to do anything to convince the Romans you're as plebeian as they are."

My mother and Menelaus enjoyed hearing those remarks as much as Lukas had making them.

"Another thing I'm leery about," I said, "in fact, the thing I'm most concerned about, is this invitation comes from a military commander, one who saw fit to invade and capture a city with no higher authority than his own to do it."

My mother nodded. "That also gives me pause."

"Thalia told us," I said, "she thinks his invasion and capture of Coriolis was his answer to Brutus and the plebeians for their grain riots. So what's his plan for me and Lukas when we become his guests in Rome?"

"You could accept his invitation," Lukas said, "go to Rome and determine for yourself what he's up to. I'd be with you, of course, to help you decide. You could always tell the people of Rome they don't need a patrician military commander acting on his own."

I laughed. "If I did that, he'd no doubt cancel his invitation and ask us to go back to Sparta."

"And," Lukas said, "having seen Rome by then, we'd book passage on Thalia's ship and come home to Sparta."

My mother, who'd tangled at my age with a powerful military commander, Agamemnon, her future brother-in-law, didn't seem persuaded.

Marco

Timon and Lukas found me in the kitchen early the next morning, nibbling on raisins and figs with Leda and Hermione.

"We're on our way to the olive grove," Lukas said. "We've got a lot of work to do today."

"Especially," Timon said, "if we're going to travel to a foreign land in the near future."

I couldn't tell if his remark was intended as sarcasm or as a hint he and Lukas might accept my father's invitation.

"You seem to be the type of person," Lukas said to me, "who can keep himself entertained."

"Don't worry about that," I said. "I'm going to the king's chamber shortly. He asked me if I'd like to work out with him this morning. I told him I'd be delighted to. I've got to keep myself active while I'm here. When I was on the ship, I decided I wasn't going to sit around and do nothing. So I asked Thalia if I could take an oar when the sailors needed to row the boat. They were surprised a paying passenger wanted to do what they did, but they got used to it. They even taught me how to help them raise and take down the sails."

My remarks appeared to amuse Lukas. "I take it," he said, "you're not a typical Roman patrician."

I shrugged. "I've never wondered whether I was or wasn't."

Marco

When I set out for Greece, I hadn't imagined I'd lift weights and jump rope with the king of Sparta. He told me he and Helen used his chamber only for keeping fit and reading and writing documents for their work as king and queen. When they wanted to relax, they went to her chamber. Helen was in another room in Menelaus's chamber then going over some documents needing their approval.

I laid down the weights I'd been using. "Do Timon and Lukas work out with you here?"

"In the winter," Menelaus replied, "when they're not busy in the olive grove. For a long time now, I've considered them my sons."

He laid down the weights he'd been lifting.

"I'd like to know more about your father," he said. "I understand his navy and army captured a city a neighboring kingdom claimed it should rule."

"That's what my father did," I said.

"I also understand," Menelaus said, "the people of Rome so admired what he did they gave him the name he goes by now."

I nodded. "His warriors and sailors insisted on it."

"But in the stories I've heard, your father fought the battle without seeking prior approval from the Roman senate or consul."

"He had to do that. The Volscian kingdom was gathering its army on its side of the city. My father knew their warriors were going to enter the city as soon as their army reached its full strength. After they took the city, it would've been much more difficult for our army to capture it. The Volscian archers would've been on top of its walls firing their arrows down at us. My father decided he couldn't afford to wait while the senate and the consul dithered about what to do next. He needed to act."

Menelaus had carefully listened to every word I'd said. "I was told the Volscians had promised the Roman consul and senate they wouldn't invade the city as long as their negotiations continued."

"My father didn't think that promise amounted to much, not while the Volscians were bringing every warrior they had to their side of the border with the city."

"Were you with your father," Menelaus asked, "when the battle for Coriolis took place?"

"I was. I'd turned eighteen by then. So I was old enough to fight with the army. My father and I were in the front line of our warriors. We helped smash down the main gate. We were among the first warriors to enter the city. To tell you the truth, though, after our navy destroyed the city's fleet in its harbor, the warriors inside its walls did little more than retreat and surrender. The Roman navy won that battle. Those of us fighting on the ground suffered very few casualties."

Chapter Four

Timon

Later that morning, Marco and Menelaus came running together on the path through the olive grove, both of them wearing nothing but a loincloth. When they passed Lukas and me and the other workers, Marco joined the king in giving each of us a vigorous wave of his hand.

Lukas and I climbed down from the tree we'd finished pruning and took a break in the shade of the next tree we planned to work on.

Lukas turned to me and shrugged. "If we accept the invitation, we'll be doing Marco a big favor."

"So he can claim," I asked, "he's done what his war-commander father wanted him to do?"

"Not just that. He'll be the person who's brought the only living member of the Trojan royal family to Rome to meet the other survivors of the fall of Troy and their families. The people might be pleased with him for doing it."

"On the other hand, the people who've chosen a republic for their form of government might not be pleased to have a member of their former royal family appear among them. They might wish he'd stay away—maybe in the idyllic land known as Sparta, where the king and queen, unlike almost all other kings and queens, have chosen to be kind to the people they're responsible for."

Lukas shook his head. "The only child of Paris and Helen could also go to Rome for a good reason."

"What would that be?"

"He could tell the people he supports their republican form of government and has no wish to claim any right he might've had under the monarchy they wisely abolished. The people might love Marco for bringing him to Rome to let them know, face-to-face, where he stands."

I took my eyes off Menelaus and Marco, who were running

toward the royal apple orchard, and turned to Lukas. "You like Marco."

Lukas didn't hesitate. "So do you. I could see he had his knee up against your thigh under the table last night. And you let him do it."

"And I could see he also had his other knee up against your thigh."

Lukas laughed. "So he did. He put his long legs to good use. But neither of us did anything to make him think we didn't want him to continue doing what he was doing."

"Whatever happened last night," I said, "I don't think liking Marco is a reason to go to Rome with him. We'll have to learn to like him at a distance. I'm sure we'll figure out how to do it. We can always invite him to visit Sparta again. Everybody here seems to be as fond of him as we are. He's running almost naked with the king. I think we can ask him to pay us another visit."

Lukas looked in the direction of the apple orchard. I doubted, though, he was focusing his attention on the swollen buds on the trees, ready to break into bloom and dazzle the world once more.

Then he turned to me again. "No, I don't think our lust for Marco is a good reason to pay a visit to Rome. But going there and setting matters straight is a damned good reason."

"What do mean, *setting matters straight?*"

"Everybody knows who you are now. You're the long-lost son of Paris and Helen, no less. You don't really have a right to hide out in an olive orchard in Sparta and pretend you're a nobody. I think you have a duty to go to Rome and let the people there know, from your own mouth, two things."

"What two things?"

"First, you have absolutely no wish to rule Rome or any other land."

"That's true. I can honestly tell them that. What's next?"

"You're in full agreement with their wish to be a republic. You also think most kingdoms—all those without a Menelaus for a king and a Helen for queen—would be better off as republics, where every last person eighteen years and older has the right to vote."

"I can say something like that."

"I think you should say something like that. The Romans are your father's people."

Marco

After my second evening meal in Sparta, I once again helped the king and queen and the other four residents of the palace wash, dry and put away the dishes. When we were done, we gathered in Helen's chamber to drink the sweet wine they favored, especially after their supper.

Lukas sang a song he'd composed. He accompanied himself with a lyre. Timon played a pan flute.

> *From Agamemnon's war we fled*
> *Together in a seaborne bed.*
> *A king and queen had saved our lives.*
> *They took us to a land that thrives*
> *On reason now. At that time, though,*
> *They couldn't let their people know*
> *You were a prince, an enemy*
> *Whose innocence took years to see.*

Lukas turned to Timon and, for a chorus, sang the last five lines a second time.

"I take it," I said, "the song explains why we survivors of Troy didn't know until recently our prince was alive."

"The song explains that," Helen said. "Menelaus and I agreed Timon would have to decide for himself, after he became an adult, whether he should reveal his identity to the world."

I turned to Timon. "And you decided to do that."

Timon nodded. "The day I turned eighteen. Thanks to Menelaus and my mother, Sparta is, as Lukas says, a land that thrives on reason now."

Marco

After the musical interlude, Timon had some news for his family and me. "The workers in the olive grove have agreed Lukas and I can take some time off. They believe they'll be able to handle everything that needs to be done in our absence."

Helen, Menelaus, Leda and Hermione couldn't conceal their apprehension.

"You've decided to visit Rome?" Helen asked Timon.

I didn't dare let Timon's family know I was as joyful as they were fearful.

Timon nodded. "Lukas and I will go with Marco on Thalia's next ship to Rome. She told us it'll depart two days from now."

"I thought," Timon's mother said, "you were wary of doing that. You worried the Romans might think you'd claim a right to be their king."

"I'm going to Rome," Timon said, "to make it clear to every Roman who wishes to hear me I have no desire to be their king."

"Every last Roman," I said, "will wish to hear and see you. You survived the war, the same as they did. Nobody will pass up the opportunity to meet you."

"You could send them a message," Menelaus said, "a document signed by you renouncing any right you might have to be their king. Marco could take it with him. Your mother and I could countersign it to authenticate your signature."

Timon shook his head. "I wish to look the Romans in their eyes when I tell them I have no interest in being their king. I want to go further. I want to let them know I fully agree they should rule themselves in a republic. I also want them to know I fervently hope for their success.

I want to tell them all how I feel person-to-person. I don't want to hide here in Greece and send messages to them."

Menelaus turned to me. "Thalia has told us political matters in republican Rome can become extremely contentious. She says candidates for your senate and consulship have gone so far as to murder their opponents."

Timon responded to those remarks before I had a chance to.

"I can assure you," he said, "I'll never be a candidate for the Roman senate or consulship. I intend to make that very clear. Neither will I support or oppose any of the persons who'll be candidates for those positions. I want them to know I consider myself a Greek now, and I always will. I've very happily lived in Greece for all but the first year of my life. I can't imagine why any Romans would want to kill me."

I turned to Menelaus and Helen, who sat close to one another on a couch. Their story was true. From the day they'd met in the orphanage walnut grove, they'd been in love.

"I can also assure you," I said, "both Timon and Lukas will be under the protection of my father every moment they're on Roman soil. They'll be there as his guests. And my father is, as you know, the commander of Rome's army and navy. Timon and Lukas will be as safe and secure in Rome as they are here in Sparta."

"That will be a hard order to fill," Leda said.

Menelaus and Helen had placed her in charge of selling the produce from the palace grounds. Any goods she didn't sell she gave to Spartans who couldn't afford to pay anything for them.

"We haven't had a murder in Sparta," she said, "for at least ten years now. We have my daughter and son-in-law to thank for that. They've carefully kept the peace in this land."

Hermione turned to me. "Will you help protect Timon and Lukas during their visit to your city?"

"As a warrior in my father's army," I said, "I'm sworn to protect any rightful guests in Rome, and certainly any guests of his."

Hermione, the heir to her father's throne, nodded. "We'll worry about Timon and Lukas every day they're gone. We and Sparta, you know, love them dearly."

"I've learned that," I said. "I promise you I'll do whatever it takes to keep them safe."

Marco

Timon sang a song he'd composed. This time he played the lyre, and Lukas played the pan flute.

> *A king decided on a war*
> *To make his reputation soar*
> *In history. His monstrous strife*
> *Ensnared our kin but gave us life.*
> *It gave you me. It gave me you.*
> *It made us pause and look it through.*
> *However much we understand,*
> *It took us to a peaceful land.*

Timon turned to Lukas and repeated his last four lines as a chorus.

Chapter Five

Marco

I began to wonder if I could defy my father and tell Timon and Lukas they should remain in Sparta. Menelaus was right. Rome wasn't a peaceful land.

I even tried to imagine living in Sparta myself. I'd gladly work in the olive grove, taking my orders from Timon and Lukas.

But I had to resist daydreaming. My father would never let me do it. He'd send ships with warriors in them to get me. I couldn't ask Helen and Menelaus to defy him and refuse to hand me over. That was the tragic mistake the Trojans had made.

Timon

All seven of us rode together in a carriage to the harbor. I'd volunteered to sit on the floor between the seats. Lukas was on my left. Marco, who'd chosen to wear nothing under his tunic that day, was on my right.

After Lukas, Marco and I walked up the gangplank to Thalia's ship, I turned and looked back at my mother, stepfather, sister and grandmother. They tried their best to appear cheerful as they waved goodbye to us, but I knew they had doubts. I had my own, imagining Lukas and I were boaters in a stream new to us approaching a hidden waterfall.

I turned again and saw Thalia standing near the foremast, herself waving goodbye to my family. The expression on her face, as dark as that of a mother attending the funeral of her child, was no help.

Timon

Lukas and I were as unwilling to sit out our trip to Italy as Marco was.

"I'm not surprised," Thalia said when we told her we wanted to help with the rowing and whatever other work on her ship we could learn to do. "And I'm certain my crew will have no objection."

Marco had traveled from Italy to Greece with the same crew. Lukas and I could see they'd taken to him the way we and the other residents of the palace in Sparta had. When we ate our meals with them, he revealed he'd remembered all their names and a number of amusing stories they'd shared with him involving themselves, their families and other ship crews they'd worked with.

Marco

During our voyage to Rome, Timon, Lukas and I established a routine. After we finished our work for the day and ate our evening meals, we drank wine together, usually sitting on the deck watching the sunset and the moonrise. During the evenings of two rainy days rounding the boot of Italy, though, we drank our wine in their room.

As in Sparta and on the deck, they didn't seem to mind when I let some part of my body come in contact with some part of theirs and remain in that position. But when the three of us were alone in their room on the ship, I couldn't get my mind off the possibility of our removing our clothes, taking positions on their bed and letting matters proceed from there.

But I held back from asking them to do that. I worried they'd consider me an unwanted intruder. They'd told me they'd grown up together in Queen Helen's orphanage as if they'd always known they'd become, at some point, lovers. Soon after hair started growing on their faces and bodies, and their voices changed, they proved it. I wondered if they'd ever included a third person in their love-making, but they gave me no hint they'd done so—or wished to do so.

On my previous voyage from Italy to Greece, I'd shared my bed a few times with a member of the crew a couple of years older than me.

On the return passage he let me know he wanted to resume our liaisons. He seemed to be an honest man, like Timon and Lukas, with a lean and hard body, also like theirs, and I accepted his offers. During our times together, though, I couldn't keep myself from thinking of doing with them what I was doing with him.

Timon

One evening after our work was done, Thalia asked Lukas and me to speak with her in her room. Even though she was the ship's captain, her room wasn't much larger or more elaborate than the one we occupied. She and Lukas sat on a bench. I occupied the single chair she had.

Thalia was a few years older than my mother and Menelaus. She lived in Sparta with a woman her age who was her long-time companion and business partner and often captained their other ship.

Thalia had grown up the only child of traders who bought and sold goods in the harbor in Sparta. She blamed their meager earnings, as well as their poor health leading to their early deaths, on their refusal to do what many of the other traders did—cheat on the confiscatory taxes Atreus, and later Agamemnon, saw fit to impose on trading.

"If Menelaus and Helen had been in power in Sparta when my parents did business," Thalia once told Lukas and me, "they could've at least owned a house they didn't have to share with rats."

Thalia had met her companion when they worked on a ship as apprentice sailors after they'd become adults and left their families. Her companion's parents and siblings were shepherds who tended, for wages, sheep and goats other people owned.

As soon as Lukas and I sat down in her room, Thalia revealed why she'd wished to speak with us. "I can see you both enjoy spending your time with Marco."

"I confess," I said, "we do."

"He's a very likable guy," Lukas said.

33

"The people in Rome he has the most contact with," Thalia said, "would agree with you."

"Who are they?" I asked.

"His security guards," Thalia replied. "Of course, they're carefully selected for their positions."

"Who carefully selects them?" Lukas asked.

"His father selects warriors from his army to act as Marco's security guards. They also provided his warrior training. Even now, though, after he turned eighteen and became a warrior himself, at least one of them has to accompany him whenever he wishes to go beyond the guard posts surrounding his father's house. Old Marco claims he does it for his son's protection. He worries his enemies might want to kidnap or murder his only child."

Thalia had told us not many people in Rome referred to Marco's father by his new name, Coriolanus. Almost everybody still called him Old Marco.

"Young Marco doesn't have warriors with him now," Lukas said. "He didn't have any with him in Sparta."

Thalia nodded. "This trip is the first time his father has allowed him to be on his own. I told Old Marco I doubted anybody in Greece or aboard any ship of mine would want to kidnap or murder his son. Nor would the peace-loving royal Spartan household look favorably upon playing host to armed security guards in addition to Marco. Helen and Menelaus and their family live safely, I told him, without guards. Old Marco agreed with me his son should visit Sparta by himself."

"You seem to know Old Marco rather well," I said.

Thalia nodded. "I do."

"You must speak with him privately," I said.

She nodded again. "I do."

"Why is that?" I asked.

"I do business with him," Thalia said. "I do a great deal of business with the army and navy he commands. I've sold him the finest weaponry Greek artisans produce. I've sold him the Spartan royal

34

family's grain, fruit, nuts and olive oil."

"Why does he do so much business with you?" I asked.

"He trusts me. I'm honest. I'm the child of my parents. I've never sold him, or anybody else, shoddy goods. I stand ready to take back, or make up for, anything I sell not serving its purpose. I don't overcharge, even when I know I can. He pays the same price for your olive oil he'd have to pay for any other olive oil from Greece. And I've seen his warriors and sailors smack their lips and tell me what they're tasting must've come from the royal Spartan olive grove."

"Is Old Marco honest?" I asked.

Thalia nodded. "In business matters he's honest to a fault. He's as honest as I am. That's why I deal with him as much as I do. I'll deliver half the cargo in this ship, as well as its three passengers, to him. He says honest producers and traders should rule the world."

"What about honest workers?" Lukas asked.

Thalia shook her head. "He tells me workers who do what they're asked to do should accept, without complaining, the pay they've bargained for, the same as honest producers and traders do. But workers who can't read or write or understand arithmetic and become producers or traders should have no say in running the world."

"That's his idea of a republic?" I asked.

"That's what he says," Thalia replied. "The Roman plebeians, though, have a different idea. Their leader, Brutus, has explained it for me. He believes the more numerous workers should rule the world, even if it means the producers and traders have to buy and sell their grain, olive oil and other goods for the prices the workers decide are the prices they can pay without living in misery."

Thalia could see her remarks had left Lukas and me dazed. We lived, after all, in a land ruled by a benevolent king and queen we loved. We hadn't spent much time worrying ourselves about prices. Like the other producers and traders in Greece, my mother and Menelaus sold the products from their palace grounds for whatever they could get for them.

They made one royal exception to that general rule, though. If they thought the price they could get for whatever they were selling didn't adequately reimburse them for the cost of producing it, they gave it away to the people who lacked the silver and gold to pay anything for it.

My mother and Menelaus appeared to know what they were doing. Lukas and I had seen for ourselves how much silver and gold they had in their vault in the palace basement. Unlike many Greek kings and queens, they never borrowed from the lenders. They could afford to be benevolent.

Lukas interrupted my thoughts with a question for Thalia. "You say Old Marco is as honest as you are in business matters. But what about other matters? Such as political matters?"

Thalia nodded. "You've made my point. Old Marco feels no need for honesty when it comes to matters other than business matters. And that's why you have to be very careful when you arrive in Rome."

"What in particular," I asked, "do you think we should be careful about?"

Thalia turned to me and frowned. "I feel certain Old Marco has a reason of his own for inviting the last surviving member of the Trojan monarchy and his companion to republican Rome. Sometime during your visit, you'll find out what that reason is. I doubt you'll learn he invited you and Lukas to Rome for his son's entertainment—even if that's not something he'd object to."

"Entertainment?" Lukas asked.

A bystander who didn't know Thalia might've said the look she gave Lukas was a smirk. "Are you hoping for love?"

Chapter Six

Marco

As Thalia's ship sailed up the western coast of Italy, my Spartan friends had numerous questions for me about Rome. One sunny morning when we and the sailors had no rowing or work with the sails to do, Timon and Lukas focused on the grain riots.

"What were they all about?" Timon asked.

"The plebeians claimed," I said, "they were paying too much for wheat and barley."

We stood at the rail on the landward side of ship as we waited for the call to eat the midday meal with the crew below the deck.

"Weren't some of the plebcians starving?" Lukas asked.

"My father told me that wasn't true," I said. "They weren't dying of starvation. The usual number of them were dying for the reasons people die all the time."

"We heard," Timon said, "they were suffering a famine."

I shook my head. "Some of the plebeians tried to make that claim. My father told me it was a lie. There was no famine. The plebeians had simply decided the prices they were paying for wheat and barley were higher than they wanted to pay. Nobody could blame them for that. Grain prices are important to them. Bread and beer are mostly what they eat and drink. But they weren't starving."

"Had they rioted before," Lukas asked, "over the grain prices?"

"Nobody," I said, "could remember them doing that."

Lukas was persistent. "So why did they riot then?"

I was more than a little irritated by the questions Timon and Lukas chose to ask me. It was a sunny day with a favorable breeze from the south filling the sails, and they wanted to talk about those damned grain riots.

I envisioned them and me taking off our clothes and doing what

I wanted us to do, even as the members of the crew chose to turn away disgusted or watch delighted.

"Brutus inflamed the people," I replied instead. "My father says that's all he's good for. He's an excellent orator. There's no question about that. He can bring tears to the eyes of people with hearts as hard as stone. He can wax sarcastic and provoke people to laugh until it hurts too much to laugh anymore. He can also make people angry and incite them to violence. That's what he did during the grain riots."

"Have you heard him speak yourself?" Timon asked.

I nodded. "I've heard him speak. He puts on a show for the people. He appeals to their prejudice against the patricians."

"You don't think he's telling the people the truth?" Timon asked.

He and Lukas kept throwing questions at me as if they were inquisitors the consul had sent to hear me confess I'd committed a heinous crime.

"I know Brutus isn't telling the truth," I said. "My father can poke a big hole in every argument he makes."

Lukas wouldn't stop. "You talk a lot about these things with your father?"

"My father wants to keep me informed," I said. "I'm the only child he's ever had. He spends a lot of time with me. My warrior friends tell me their fathers would never spend that much time with them. I feel very fortunate to have the father I have."

Timon and Lukas looked at one another as if the story I'd told them might make them weep. Then I realized the mistake I'd made. I should've kept my mouth shut. They couldn't remember their fathers doing anything with them, not even holding them in their arms.

After we heard the call to lunch, though, they turned to me and laughed.

Lukas extended an arm around my waist. "I'm damned ready for some more fish-and-onion soup. I bet you are too."

Timon, on the other side of me, threw an arm around my

shoulders and sniffed the air in the direction of the hole we had to drop ourselves through to reach the space with narrow benches and tables where we ate. "I'm ready for the bread they're taking out of the oven right now."

Timon

"Do you believe it's possible," Lukas asked Marco, after we'd finished the midday meal and returned to the deck, "your father doesn't always tell you the truth?"

"I don't know why he'd do that," Marco replied. "My father wants me, of all people, to know the truth. He's grooming me to be second to him in command of the Roman army and navy, and his successor when he retires or dies. He tells me persons who don't know the facts about the people they live with can never fill a position such as his. No, I'm confident he wouldn't lie to me."

The wind had died while we were eating lunch. The ship had stalled.

"It's time to help row this boat," Lukas said.

Marco seemed relieved he wouldn't have to discuss his father any further.

Timon

The following day we reached the harbor at Ostia, where the River Tiber met the sea. The city of Rome was upriver northeast of the harbor. But traders from foreign lands couldn't go there. They needed to unload and reload their ships at Ostia.

Marco, Lukas and I said our reluctant goodbyes to Thalia and her crew and made our way down the gangplank.

Ten warriors with swords and daggers in leather sheaths strapped to their bodies stood on the dock.

"They're our guards," Marco said.

Lukas looked them up and down. "Warriors from the guard posts surrounding your father's house?"

The question surprised Marco. "How'd you find out about the guard posts?"

"Thalia told us," Lukas replied.

"Why so many guards?" I asked.

"My father," Marco said, "doesn't take any chances. He doesn't want any harm done to his son or his guests from Sparta."

The warriors were as friendly toward Marco as the sailors on Thalia's ship had been. I assumed they considered guarding their commander's son and house an honor.

They accompanied Marco, Lukas and me to a carriage.

The captain of all the guards at the posts surrounding Old Marco's house climbed aboard it after we did. She told Lukas and me her name was Livia.

Eight warriors rode in chariots, four preceding and four following us. The remaining warrior drove the two horses pulling the carriage.

"Where are we going?" Lukas asked.

"To my father's estate," Marco replied. "It's east of here and south of the city of Rome. It won't take us long to get there."

Marco

I couldn't help but notice the apprehension of Timon and Lukas. They weren't used to being accompanied by armed warriors in Sparta.

"They're with us," I said, "for our protection."

"I'd hoped," Lukas said, "we wouldn't need this much protection."

Livia, who sat on the back seat of the carriage with Timon facing Lukas and me on the front seat, laughed. "Welcome to Rome."

Timon

Who Killed Coriolanus?

Livia appeared to me to be about the same age as my mother and Menelaus. And, like them, she was fit. She must've spent as much of her time training as Marco and the other warriors did.

We passed fields of wheat and barley.

"These are my father's," Marco said.

"The people who manage his fields," Livia said, "tell me they're pleased we've had so much rain this spring. They hope the season's yields will be outstanding."

"The workers will like that," Marco said. "If they make sure it all gets harvested after it ripens but before it starts to fall off the stalks, my father will give them bonuses."

Lukas turned to Marco. "Does your father sell his wheat to the plebeians?"

Livia grimaced when she heard the last word of that question.

"No," Marco said. "My father sells all the products from his estate to traders, and they sell them to the people who consume them."

"So I imagine," Lukas said, "your father wants to keep the grain prices high."

Marco shrugged. "All the people who grow wheat and barley want high prices for them. The people who don't own fields of grain want the prices low. That's the way the world is."

"And your senators," I said, "set the prices."

Marco nodded. "They're required to set fair prices. They take a vote on them every year, after the harvest."

I knew Lukas wouldn't let Marco get away with the *fair prices* in those remarks. "But don't the patricians who grow the grain and the plebeians who consume it have very different views on what a fair price is? Isn't that also the way the world is?"

Marco glanced at Livia and decided not to pursue the matter any further. He shrugged instead. "I guess so."

The trail entered a fruit orchard.

"Does this belong to your father?" I asked Marco.

He nodded. "I told you my father owns one of largest estates in

Rome. His family's grain and livestock kept the Trojans alive during the war. Your grandparents Priam and Hecuba, and your uncle Hector, promised them they'd be appropriately rewarded when the war was over. The survivors of the war made good on that promise when we reached Italy."

Marco's references to the war darkened Livia's expression as if unseen clouds had somehow obliterated that day's relentless blue sky. I wondered what role she'd played in the fighting that took my father's life.

Marco

After I mentioned Timon's grandparents and uncle in the carriage, I realized he and I could've grown up together if Agamemnon and the other Greek kings hadn't gone to war to take his mother back to Sparta. I could've been in the same position Lukas was. I could've turned eighteen sharing a chamber with Timon in the palace in Troy, or he could've lived with me in my family's house in the country. My mother and his father might still be alive too.

But I was daydreaming again for no good purpose. My actual life offered hope enough. Timon and Lukas and I were headed to the house I lived in. My father would be as pleased as I was I'd talked them into coming home with me.

The many questions Timon and Lukas had asked me regarding my father had irritated me at first but eventually increased my admiration for them. They chose for themselves the course they took through life.

One of the choices they'd made was to spend more time with me. And I was certain their family and friends in Sparta—especially Helen, Menelaus, Hermione, Leda and Thalia—hadn't wanted them to do that if it included sailing to Rome.

Chapter Seven

Timon

The carriage passed through a village.

"Who lives here?" Lukas asked.

"The workers on my father's estate," Marco replied. "They live in their houses for free. My father doesn't charge them any rent. Most landlords do."

Before we reached the dwelling Marco and his father lived in, I'd anticipated it would be a sumptuous villa, but it wasn't that at all.

It was a plain and simple house not unlike some of those we passed in the village. When Marco took Lukas and me inside it, we could see its rooms weren't built with the entertainment of crowds of guests in mind.

Lukas couldn't let his surprise go to waste. "I take it," he said, "this is the guesthouse Timon and I will be staying in. Where's the house you and your father live in?"

I had no doubt Lukas was being facetious.

Marco laughed. "This is the house my father and I live in. I should've told you. He's personally frugal. The reason he booked passage for us on Thalia's ship was the price she'd asked him to pay for it."

I assumed Thalia had made certain her price was the lowest.

Timon

As we walked from room to room, Marco continued telling us about his father with far greater enthusiasm than he had on the ship. "He's never been willing to settle for the paltry tax money the senators have been willing to raise for the army and navy. Over the years he's spent a large amount of his own silver and gold keeping the forces in the numbers he thinks they should be and with the arms and other equipment he thinks they should have."

Marco took Lukas and me to the second floor of his father's house and showed us the room we'd be sleeping in during our visit. Marco told us it was the only room in the house available for guests. Marco and his father also had bedrooms on the second floor.

"Where do your servants sleep?" Lukas asked.

"They have a bedroom on the first floor," Marco said. "It's near the kitchen."

"Your servants all sleep in one room?" Lukas asked.

Marco laughed again. "Both of our servants sleep in one bed in one room. They grew up in Troy with my father. They were sons of workers on the land my father's family owned there."

"They're brothers?" Lukas asked.

I often wondered if other people found Lukas's inquisitiveness as invasive as it sometimes seemed to me. I thought it was highly unlikely two men the same age as Marco's father who slept in one bed would be brothers. I was also pleased, though, Lukas's curiosity led to so many answers to questions I had no need to ask myself.

Marco shook his head.

"They're lifelong companions?" Lukas persisted.

"They are," Marco replied.

Marco

I took Timon and Lukas down to the kitchen. Domenic and Philo were preparing the evening meal, but they stopped their work as soon as they looked up and saw our two guests from Greece.

"Which one of you," Domenic asked, "is the long-lost son of Paris and Helen we've heard so much about lately?"

I put one hand Timon's shoulder. "This is Timon." I placed my other hand on Lukas's shoulder. "And this is his companion, Lukas."

I nodded toward Domenic and then Philo as I revealed their names to Timon and Lukas and completed the introductions.

Domenic stared at Timon. "There isn't a person in Rome who

44

doesn't want to meet you. We'd all given up hoping you'd survived. Then, out of the blue, Thalia assured us you were alive and well in Sparta with your mother the queen and your stepfather the king."

Philo also stared at Timon. "And here you are, in person."

Domenic laughed. "He and his companion both seem very alive and well, don't they?"

"They certainly do," Philo agreed.

Domenic couldn't take his eyes off Timon. "I must say your mother's story is remarkable. She was supposed to marry the king of Sparta. Instead, she sailed to Troy with Paris. She married him and had a child with him, you. Then, after the war she returned to Greece and married Menelaus, and he accepted you as his stepson. You'll have to fill us in on all the details of that story."

I shook my head. "I'm not sure we can expect Timon to answer questions about his mother's personal life."

"Oh, no," Timon said. "I'm perfectly willing to answer any questions you have about my mother."

"She doesn't have anything to conceal," Lukas said. "She laid out all the facts of her life for Timon and me."

"She tells us," Timon said, "she loved the Trojan people. She's always been very sorry Agamemnon and the other Greek kings started the war. She considers the destruction of the beautiful city of Troy one of the most evil deeds of all time."

"Did you know," Philo asked, "after she and Paris married, Hector, Priam and Hecuba put her in charge of all the orchards, vineyards, groves and gardens in Troy?"

Timon nodded. "She told us that."

"She was considered an expert horticulturist," Philo said.

"She still is," Lukas said. "The palace orchards, groves and vineyards are the most productive in Sparta. She's brought that about. And she does it for the Spartan people. All the profit goes to them one way or another."

Domenic turned to Timon again. "We saw you once. Marco's

father was fighting on the frontline. We were running errands for him and his comrades, hoping we wouldn't get hit by a Greek arrow. Your mother was on a rooftop holding a shield for your father. He was the best archer the Trojans had. She was holding another shield for herself and you. You were on her lap sleeping through the uproar of the battle."

"I was probably used to it by then," Timon said.

Timon

Lukas, Marco and I drank wine in the courtyard from plain ceramic cups.

"Plebeians," Marco had told us when he poured our wine, "drink beer from cups like these."

The courtyard was open to the south. Narcissuses, hyacinths and forsythias were in bloom.

"Who does the gardening?" Lukas asked.

"Domenic," Marco replied. "I help him whenever he asks me to. I learned many years ago to tell the difference between weeds and flowers in his gardens."

Marco's father came out of the house and entered the courtyard. Marco had told us he'd probably spent that day as he did most of his days, in training with his warriors or sailors.

He was a few years older than my mother and Menelaus. As he approached us, I could see his training had kept him as physically desirable as they were. I could also see the fathers of Lukas and me might've looked very much like him.

"I know who you are," Old Marco said to me and turned to Lukas. "And you must be Timon's Spartan companion. Domenic and Philo tell me they have our evening meal ready for us."

Timon

The only furnishings in the dining room were a round wooden

table with six wooden chairs. Marco and his father sat down opposite one another.

Marco gestured to Lukas and me to sit on either side of him.

There were cups, plates and utensils on the table where the two remaining chairs stood.

"Will Domenic and Philo," Lukas asked, "eat with us?"

"They will," Marco replied.

The walls of the room were decorated with paintings as colorful as the flowers in the courtyard. Similar landscapes, seascapes and still lifes appeared on the walls of the other rooms and hallways in the house.

"Who does the artwork?" Lukas asked.

"Philo," Marco replied. "He does the indoor art. Domenic does the outdoor kind."

"Lovely in both cases," Lukas said.

I turned to Marco's father. "Did you know my father in Troy?"

Old Marco nodded. "I knew your father. To be honest with you, though, he and I weren't close. I came in contact with your uncle Hector far more often than I did your father. I spent my days then much as I do now—training with the warriors. I can't recall your father ever spending so much as one day training to become a warrior. He chose instead to be an athlete. He spent his time preparing for the games. He was, no question about it, an outstanding athlete. Many people argued he was the best who'd ever competed in our games. I had no reason to doubt they were right. The people loved him. Then he brought your mother to Troy and changed the course of history for both Greece and Troy."

"Neither my mother nor my father," I said, "voluntarily chose to sail to Troy together. Agamemnon forced them to do it."

Old Marco nodded again. "That's the story we hear now. And I have no doubt it's true. It was the sort of thing Agamemnon did."

Domenic brought into the dining room a carafe of wine to fill our cups.

Philo set down in the middle of the table a ceramic platter of appetizers. He'd nestled thumbnail-size pieces of fish and goat cheese

47

crumbs in cuts of red and yellow onions and left them in the oven only as long as it took to cook the fish and melt the cheese.

"The onions," Marco said, "came from the garden Domenic and Philo keep."

"The fish," Domenic said, "came from the market in the village."

"Domenic and Philo," Marco said, "made the goat cheese."

After Domenic and Philo sat down and Lukas and Marco began helping themselves to the appetizers, Old Marco turned to me.

"Your father surprised us," he said. "He was damned good at killing Greeks with his bow and arrow. He could see when they made the slightest mistake with their shields. If they gave him any opening at all, his arrows were deadly accurate. People said he killed far more Greeks than any other Trojan warrior. They were right about that, too."

Chapter Eight

Timon

Lukas, having devoured his first appetizer, chose to speak, as if to nobody in particular at the table. "Some of the Greeks Timon's father killed were workers like my mother and father. They weren't warriors. They had no reason or desire to invade Troy and kill the people who lived there. What difference did it make to them if a Trojan prince had run off with an orphan woman who was supposed to marry the Spartan king? A king can easily find some other person to share his bed with. But Agamemnon forced my parents and all those other workers to go to Troy. He ordered his warriors to kill anybody who resisted."

Old Marco shook his head. "In a war everybody on the other side is fair game. You can't ask warriors to decide who wants to be fighting for the enemy and who doesn't. If people choose to surrender themselves, I think it's right to take them prisoner and at least try to keep them alive until the war is over. It makes good sense to do that. People are much more likely to surrender if they know their enemy keeps prisoners alive. But warriors in a battle have to make every attempt to kill anybody else who's aiding the enemy, no matter why their doing it."

Old Marco once again turned to me.

Assuming he wanted a response to his remarks, I shrugged. I saw no point in making any argument for or against the brutal logic of war.

"Your father could've saved Troy," Old Marco said. "We didn't know it until after the war, though. Then we learned he'd figured out the Greeks were digging a tunnel all the way from their headquarters tent at the harbor to, and under, the main gate to Troy."

"My mother told Lukas and me what she knew about that," I said. "She was present when Paris told Hector why he believed the Greeks were digging a tunnel. But Hector told my father the tunnel existed only in his imagination. My mother told Hector he was making a mistake. She thought he couldn't admit he'd been wrong in assuming Troy, with its gigantic walls and watchtowers, was impregnable. Hector also ordered my father and mother not to speak a word about a tunnel to anybody else. That's why you and the Trojan people didn't learn until after the war what your commander had done."

I couldn't take my eyes off Old Marco. I wondered how he'd respond to my reference to a military commander—Hector, no less—making an error leading to a devastating defeat.

Old Marco nodded. "Hector's blunder was tragic. The whole war turned on it. That's why I believe it's so important to have the right person in charge of things. It's also why I'm convinced these elections in Rome are such a bad idea. Nobody teaches the people how to lead a country. So how can we expect them to choose the right person to do it?"

Timon

After Domenic and Philo removed the empty appetizer platter and returned to the kitchen, Marco looked across the table at his father. "I'm taking Timon and Lukas to the city tomorrow."

"I'm glad to hear that," his father said. "The people will be thrilled to see the long-lost son of Paris and Helen."

"Shouldn't I go incognito?" I asked.

Marco laughed. "Why on earth wouldn't we let the people know who you are?"

"Your people," I replied, "have chosen a republic as their form of government. I don't want them to think I've come here to claim my right as the last surviving member of the Trojan royal family—my right to be their king and overthrow their republic."

Marco's father scoffed. "You needn't worry about that. The people know you're here only for a visit. In their eyes, you're a tourist. A damned interesting one, with Paris for a father and Helen for a mother, but a tourist nevertheless."

Who Killed Coriolanus?

"The people already know," I asked, "I'm here?"

Marco laughed again. "When they see you and Lukas with me tomorrow, they'll know one of you is Timon, and the other is his companion. All I'll have to do is tell them which of you is which. They know I went to Sparta to invite you both to visit Rome. As soon as we walked down the gangplank from Thalia's ship this morning, I'm certain word went out the two of you had, at long last, set foot on Roman soil."

I looked across the table at Lukas, who glanced back at me and shrugged. I doubted Thalia would believe Old Marco had invited us to Rome just to show us off and make the people feel good seeing the son of Paris and Helen and his companion in person.

Marco

After we finished the evening meal, I asked Timon and Lukas to drink their after-dinner wine with me in the courtyard.

We sat on a bench. And, once again, I made sure I ended up in the middle.

"Your father," Lukas said, "is a damned good-looking man. Has he ever considered remarriage? Or does he prefer men?"

I shook my head. "Domenic and Philo assure me my father has never slept with another person since my mother died. I'm certain they'd know if he had."

"Why would your father choose such a life?" Timon asked. "He was still quite young when your mother died. I agree with Lukas. There must be a lot of people who'd be pleased to share his bed. But in all that time since the war, it hasn't happened even once?"

"Not even once," I said. "He told me himself the war was an important turning point in his life. During the course of it, he married my mother, she gave birth to me, he saw with his own eyes the great heroes take one another down, my mother got killed, and he learned your father could've saved Troy if Hector hadn't stopped him. He vowed he'd make certain nothing like that would happen to our people again. He has no need to share his bed with another person. He says he'd be wasting his time. He has more important things to attend to."

Marco

As we'd done before, Timon, Lukas and I were sitting so close together I could rub both of my knees against their thighs. And, once again, they let me do it.

I couldn't wait any longer. "I've got a question I've wanted to ask you guys from the moment I met you in Sparta. I just hope you don't think I'm being nosy if I ask it."

"If I were you," Lukas said, "I'd ask the question, nosy or not."

Timon laughed. "Lukas is the nosiest person in the world. I still love him."

"Okay," I said. "Have you ever shared a bed with a third person?"

Timon and Lukas looked at one another and grinned.

Then Lukas turned to me. "Timon and I have never shared a bed with another person. Would you like to be the first to do that?"

I took a deep breath. "Hell yes I would. I'd consider it an honor."

"Now?" Lukas asked.

"Now," I said and looked at Timon. "Do you agree?"

He laughed again. "I couldn't agree more."

Marco

I took them up to my room.

Lukas laughed as soon as he saw my bed.

"It's more than big enough," he said, "for the three of us."

"Growing up," I said, "I insisted on a big bed. Domenic and Philo told me a bed this size was a scandal, but they helped me build it anyway. They at least agreed for some people it might be handy to have."

Who Killed Coriolanus?

"But you've shared this bed," Lukas asked, "with only one other person?"

"Only one," I said.

Timon began removing his clothes.

Lukas and I wrapped our arms around each other and kissed.

After Timon was naked and in obvious need, he and I embraced and kissed as Lukas shed his clothes.

While I removed my clothes, they hugged and kissed one another, but they kept their eyes on me.

They spent their first night in Rome with me in my oversize bed. I decided my trip to Sparta and home again was a splendid success.

Timon

The next morning Marco decided we should run to the city.

"We ran farther than that in Sparta," he said.

"We'll have to carry our clothes," Lukas said. "Or do you think we should walk around Rome in our loincloths?"

Marco laughed. "I'd be accused of shamelessly showing off my guests if we did that. But my father's warriors can bring our tunics, and anything else we want them to bring, in their chariots. We can put them on when we get to the city."

"Your father's warriors?" I asked. "Are they coming with us?"

Marco nodded. "My father would never let us go to the city by ourselves. He'd be far too worried somebody would try to abduct us or kill us."

"All three of us?" I asked.

Marco nodded again. "I'm his son. You and Lukas are his guests. I've told you before. Rome isn't Sparta."

Timon

A dozen of his father's warriors riding chariots, including Livia, accompanied us during our run to the city. Half of them rode ahead of us, and the other half behind us,

After we reached the main entrance to Rome on the east bank of the River Tiber, Marco, Lukas and I put on our clothes and walked into the city with ten of our guards, again including Livia. The other two remained behind with the horses and chariots.

We soon attracted the onlookers Marco had predicted we would. The number of Romans who wanted to see the long-lost son of Paris and Helen became a crowd.

Our guards formed a circle around us and removed their swords from their shields. They wouldn't let anyone come near us.

After we entered a shady parkland, I turned to Livia.

"I'd like to stop here for a bit," I said.

Our guards, whose faces and bare legs glistened with sweat as if they'd been caught in a rain shower, came to a halt without waiting for a response from their captain.

Chapter Nine

Timon

The crowd had questions for us.

"Which one of you is Timon?" someone asked.

Marco wrapped an arm around my shoulders. "This is Timon," he said.

"Timon," the same person in the crowd shouted, "do you like being with your people again?"

"I like being in Rome," I replied. "I've liked all the Romans I've met here."

"Including your host?" someone else asked.

"My companion Lukas and I," I said, "especially like Marco."

Lukas chose that moment to wrap an arm around Marco's shoulders.

"What about Old Marco?" another person in the crowd asked.

"We're grateful to him," I said, "for his invitation to see you and your city."

"Do you intend to stay here permanently?" another person in the still-growing crowd asked.

"No," I said, "Lukas and I are only here for a visit. Our home is in Sparta, and it will always be in Sparta."

"We've heard you grew up in a Greek orphanage," somebody said. "How did you like that?"

Lukas answered the question for me. "His mother, Queen Helen of Sparta, was in charge of the orphanage. She made certain every child in it, including me, whose mother and father were shepherds, was well-fed, well-housed and well-educated. Who could ask for more?"

I nodded in agreement with everything Lukas said.

Other Romans had questions concerning the aftermath of the war in Greece.

"Is it true Helen married Menelaus the same day she returned to

Sparta?"

"That was the day they married," I replied.

"Is it true your aunt Clytemnestra's lover stabbed Agamemnon to death with a butcher knife in his bath?"

"That was how her lover chose to murder Agamemnon," I said.

"And your cousin Orestes sentenced his own mother to die for her part in the assassination?"

"He also sentenced her to die," I said, "for her blatant bribe-taking during the war."

"You're talking about your aunt Clytemnestra?"

"My mother's sister, yes."

"So why do you want to live in Greece?"

I'd guessed that question was on its way.

"We live in Sparta," I said. "My mother and Menelaus have ruled it wisely and benevolently during the seventeen years since the war. There hasn't been a single murder in that land during the last ten of those years."

"In Sparta," Lukas said, "we don't need armed guards to protect us. We go freely wherever we wish."

Timon

Like a rain long outlasting the earth's need for it, the questions from the crowd continued. The attention I received had nothing to do with anything I'd done in my life. It had everything to do with the two persons who happened to have been my mother and father—persons I wasn't aware were my mother and father before I reached the eve of my eighteenth birthday at the end of the previous summer.

I attempted, though, to be pleasant. I smiled and laughed as much as I could without appearing to be a fool. If my father hadn't thrown away his life taking down Achilles on the last day of the war in Troy, I might've lived my entire life with these people and never known Sparta.

Who Killed Coriolanus?

Marco

I saw Brutus in the distance walking toward us. He was about the same age as my father. In their youth they were probably equally attractive. At this point in his life, though, it was obvious Brutus had spent his adulthood without the rigorous daily training my father had insisted upon for himself and every other person in his army and navy.

Brutus was one of the few plebeians who could read and write and do arithmetic. Before he'd embarked upon his campaign to reform Rome's election laws , he'd been a clerk for a patrician trader, sitting at a table in the market every day keeping the records of his employer's purchases and sales. People said Brutus and his employer, unlike many other traders and their clerks, made no attempt to cheat on the trading taxes.

Brutus lived even more frugally than my father. The woman he'd married and their child both died during childbirth. He never re-married and saved a large share of his earnings. Like the patricians he claimed to despise, he'd carefully secured his silver and gold in a vault under his house only he had access to. By the time he decided to become a public figure, people who knew him said he no longer needed to work.

He reached the outer fringe of the crowd and kept walking forward. He knew the people in the crowd, who were mostly plebeians, would make way for him. He didn't stop until he came within the length of my father's warriors' swords.

He did that purposefully. He wanted to show the other plebeians he wasn't afraid of patrician warriors and their arms.

"Timon," Brutus began when the crowd fell silent, as he'd known it would, "have you come to Rome to claim your ancient right to be our king and rule us?"

I was afraid he'd ask that question.

"Since Rome is a republic," Timon replied, "I have no right to rule here. Besides, I'm not a Roman. I've lived all but the first year of my life in Sparta. My mother is the queen of Sparta. My stepfather is the king of Sparta. My companion Lukas is the son of Spartan shepherds. I therefore consider myself a Spartan."

"You're the sole surviving member of the Trojan royal family," Brutus said. "You've never given up your legal right to rule the survivors of Troy. You've never formally abdicated."

"I have no need to abdicate," Timon said. "The only people in a republic who have a right to rule are those the people and their representatives elect to rule them. I've never offered myself as a candidate in an election in Rome, and I never will."

I was glad Timon spoke back to Brutus so directly. I wrapped my arm around his shoulders again.

But Timon wasn't done. "I've never had any wish to be a prince or a king," he said. "Lukas and I are happy with our lives in Sparta."

"I've been told," Brutus said, "you live in the palace with the Spartan royal family."

"We do," Timon said. "It's a palace without a single servant or guard. Lukas and I manage the royal olive grove for my mother and Menelaus. They give all the profits from it to the people. They don't spend a single piece of the silver we earn from it on themselves."

The plebeians in the crowd looked at Timon as if he were telling them a fairy tale.

Brutus wasn't done either. "I hope you realize," he said, "your host, Old Marco, who wishes to be known now as Coriolanus, is using you."

Timon blinked. "How is he using me?"

"If you don't already know," Brutus replied, "you'll soon find out. In the meantime, you might ask the young man with his arm around your shoulders. I'm sure he knows what his father is up to."

After making those remarks, Brutus turned about and walked back through the crowd the way he'd come.

"Marco," somebody in the crowd yelled, "how is your father using his royal guest?"

"My father," I said, "isn't using either of his guests. He simply invited them to visit Rome. He's only their host as long they're here. He has no plans for them beyond that."

I felt like telling the crowd they should know by now Brutus would say and do anything, no matter how much trouble it caused, to attract attention to himself. Then I realized making a statement like that would only embroil Timon and Lukas in Rome's political squabbles even more than Brutus had already done—and far more than I wanted to.

Timon

The number of people the son of Paris and Helen attracted and their endless questions kept Lukas and me from seeing much of Rome. Livia and I agreed to end our tour.

After we left the city, she took us to a wooded area we could rest in. We and our guards sat in the shade and ate the food Domenic and Philo had packed for us and washed it down with water from a nearby well. The horses pulling the guards' chariots chomped on the grass in a sunlit glade.

Well into our meal of barley bread, goat cheese and garden greens with olive oil and vinegar, Lukas asked Marco the question I was waiting for. "What was Brutus talking about? What makes him think your father is using Timon?"

Marco didn't hesitate. "I don't have the slightest idea. Brutus is a person who'll say anything on the spur of the moment if he thinks it will get him attention. I could see he hadn't anticipated Timon wouldn't play the game he wanted to play today."

"What game was that?' Lukas asked.

"I'm certain," Marco replied, "Brutus had hoped Timon would leave open the possibility of his claiming some right to rule under the old Trojan monarchy."

We ate our food in silence for a while. I favored thinking about the previous evening's activities in Marco's bedroom over the morning's introduction to Rome.

Then Marco turned to me. "I was so damned pleased you dismissed any possibility of claiming any right you might have had to be the king of Rome. You left Brutus with no alternative. He had to come up with something explosive before he could leave. That's why he accused my father of using you. I can't imagine what he was talking about. I suspect he didn't either, but he must've thought it sounded good when he said it."

Timon

Before we resumed our journey home, Marco, Lukas and I decided to ride in the chariots with three of our guards. Two youthful male guards easily convinced Marco and Lukas their steeds would have no difficulty pulling chariots with two occupants over the hilly countryside.

I accepted Livia's invitation to ride with her. Answering my questions, she let me know me she'd fought in the war in Troy, escaped the city when it fell and sailed with the other survivors to Italy.

"I knew your father and mother," she said. "I was in the watchtowers and on the rooftops with them. You see, I was also an archer. I'd competed with your father in the games."

"You were in the watchtowers and on the rooftops with my mother and father?"

"I was."

We had to pause our conversation. Like fearful dreams coming unbidden in the middle of the night, tears threatened to fill our eyes.

Chapter Ten

Timon

During the evening meal that day, Marco's father said he was pleased to learn I'd denied I had any intention to claim any right I might've had to be the king of Rome. He used his knife to slice off his next helping of roast beef from the mound of meat on the platter Domenic had positioned in front of him, "Brutus," he said, "wanted to pick a fight with you because you're my guest."

"Why," Lukas asked, "would that make a difference to him?"

"He hates me," Old Marco replied. "And with good reason. I'm the one patrician who's more popular among the plebeians than he is."

"The plebeians admire you," Lukas asked, "because you won the battle at Coriolis?"

Old Marco nodded. "Brutus will never win a battle. The plebeians don't fight in the wars we need to fight to maintain our home in Italy. They're happy to let the offspring of the patricians do that."

Marco

Timon and Lukas slept with me in my bed again their second night in Rome. The political maneuvering we'd encountered that day seemed to me as if it had taken place in, and perhaps made sense in, another world. It had nothing to do with the three of us.

Timon

The next morning Marco talked Lukas and me into running with him to the village and back in our loincloths.

But we could run by ourselves only as far as the first guard post. After that, Livia and three other warriors doing guard duty that day needed to accompany us in their chariots. Because we weren't leaving Old Marco's estate, though, we didn't require the squadron we had with us during our run to the city.

When we reached the village, we and the horses pulling the chariots slowed to a walk. The neighborhoods the workers lived in appeared to be mostly empty of people that time of the day. Lukas and I were pleased they were so tidy. We agreed we could imagine living in them. We were surprised the market in the center of the village was so busy. It was clean and orderly nevertheless.

"My father," Marco said, "doesn't tolerate misbehavior."

Livia chuckled. "Not one bit."

On our way back to the house we chose to walk for a while through one of the pastures Old Marco's cattle, sheep and goats roamed. Even there, though, as if the placidly grazing animals might suddenly find our intrusion in their lives offensive and mount an attack on us, our armed warrior guards accompanied us in their chariots.

Marco

"Where do the guards live?" Lukas asked.

He and Timon and I were eating our midday meal in the dining room with Domenic and Philo.

"They live on the base for active warriors," I replied.

"Do they live in barracks?" Lukas asked.

I shook my head. "They live in houses."

"How many in each house," Lukas asked.

"Usually two," I said. "They pick their housemates. Some of them choose to live with more than one other person. My father lets them decide those matters on their own."

"They're all patricians?" Timon asked.

I nodded. "They're the adult sons and daughters of the patricians. Most of those who won't inherit their family's estates remain in the army or navy as long as they're fit to do so."

"Is their base far from here?" Lukas asked.

"Not far at all," I said. "It's in a hilly area to the northeast. The property is actually part of my father's estate."

"Is that where your father spends his days?" Timon asked.

I nodded again. "He's there every day he isn't sailing on one of his navy's ships."

"If Lukas and I weren't here," Timon asked, "would you spend this day with the other active warriors on their base?"

"I would," I replied.

"Are you the only active warrior," Lukas asked, "who comes home to his father's home every evening?"

"I am," I said.

"And you're also," Lukas asked, "the only active warrior who needs all-day protection by other active warriors?"

Philo chose to answer that question for me. "Marco's father believes his enemies would jump at the chance to abduct or harm his son. He's not about to let that happen."

"His plebeian enemies?" Timon asked.

"Most of his enemies," Domenic said, "are plebeians."

"His main enemy," Timon asked, "is Brutus?"

"He's the one," Domenic agreed.

I turned to Timon and Lukas. "You're not in Sparta anymore. You're in Rome. But my father has vowed to protect you just as much as he protects me. You don't need to worry."

Timon

Domenic brought into the dining room a plain ceramic bowl filled with cut-up dates and heavy cream for our dessert. Philo followed him with an olivewood serving ladle and five smaller ceramic bowls he placed in front of each of us.

"We buy the dates at the village market," Marco said. "We pick up the cream from my father's dairy workers. They have a barn near the village where they do the milking."

Domenic sat down and looked at Marco. "Your father didn't go to the base this morning. He went to the city."

"He didn't let me know," Marco said, "he was going to do that."

"More specifically," Philo said, "he went to the Curia."

"Why did he go there?" Marco asked.

"He told us," Philo replied, "the consul will announce his retirement today."

"If you ask me," Domenic said, "the poor man has grown tired of the incessant squabbling between the plebeians and patricians. If I were in his position, I'd quit too. I'd be even more inclined to retire if I were as elderly as he is."

Marco seemed confused. "So why did my father have to go to the Curia?"

Domenic laughed. "The senate will set a date for an election."

"An election," Lukas asked, "for a new consul?"

Philo shook his head. "For a new senate. Rome is a republic. The people will elect the new senators. The new senate will vote for a new consul. As a practical matter, though, the people will be voting for the new consul. Every voter will have a choice of two candidates for a senate seat. One of the candidates will be pledged to vote for Brutus for the consulship. The other candidate will be pledged to vote for his opponent."

"When will the election take place?" I asked.

"Seven days from today," Philo replied. "That's how they always do it. They give the voters seven days to listen to the speeches and make up their minds."

"Who'll be Brutus's opponent?" Lukas asked. "A patrician?"

Domenic and Philo laughed.

"Yes," Philo replied, "he'll be a patrician."

Domenic laughed again. "The wealthiest and most powerful patrician in the land—Marco's father."

Marco let his spoon loaded with dates and cream drop back into his bowl. "My father? He's running to be the new consul?"

Domenic nodded. "He went to the Curia today to announce his candidacy. He has a slate of candidates pledged to him running for every seat. And Brutus has a slate pledged to him."

Philo turned to Marco. "Your father put together his slate secretly. He told Domenic and me what he was up to, but he warned us not to tell you until the day he made his announcement, which is today."

Domenic looked at Marco with what seemed to me a pleased expression on his face. "Your father was worried you might tell other people what he was up to. He insisted on secrecy."

"What good did the secrecy do him?" Lukas asked. "Brutus, his opponent, knew damned well he was running for consul."

Lukas's comment took Marco by surprise, but I'd come to the same conclusion. Brutus had honestly claimed Marco's father was using me. Prince Timon of Troy would be his houseguest during his run for the consulship.

Domenic laughed. "Brutus only found out yesterday he'd have an opponent in the election. The news pissed him off, needless to say. Then he heard the three of you had come to the city."

"And figured out," Lukas said, "why Marco's father had invited us to Rome."

Both Domenic and Philo laughed at that.

Marco

After I learned my father was running for consul, I had to stop eating.

Timon and Lukas, though, consumed every piece of date and drop of cream they'd ladled into their bowls. They emptied their plates and bowls during every meal. They told me they'd learned to do that in the orphanage and would probably always do it.

As soon as they finished their dates and cream, Timon looked at Lukas. "You and I have to speak privately."

I knew that last word was intended for my ears.

They went out to the courtyard and sat down on a bench in the shade.

I went up to the balcony at the other end of the courtyard, stripped down to my loincloth and began doing sit-ups and pushups in the sun. Timon and Lukas knew I was too far away from them to hear what they were saying.

When they finished their conversation, Lukas walked down to my end of the courtyard, looked up at me and asked me to join them. He and Timon wished to speak with me.

"Feel free to come as you are," he chose to add, laughing.

I was in fact too covered with sweat to put my clothes on then. I carried them with me and sat down on the bench in the space they'd left for me between them.

Chapter Eleven

Marco

Timon spoke first. "Brutus was right yesterday. Your father is using me—and the three of us—for his own purposes. He prevailed upon you to travel to Greece to invite us to Rome. Lukas and I have no doubt he was hoping we'd find you too irresistible to say no to. He knew what he was doing. And that's why we're here in Rome with you now."

"I'm no more irresistible to you," I said, "than you guys are to me."

"That might be so," Timon said. "In any event, your father knew, if you were successful in enticing us to Rome, we'd be here during his seven-day campaign for the consulship. He knew my presence as his guest would, by itself, lead the voters to think he had the backing of what was left of the royal house of Troy. That would probably count for something for at least some of the voters. Brutus was precisely right. Your father is using me."

Lukas turned to me. "Your father didn't want you to know he was running for consul. If you'd known, you would've figured out why he wanted Timon in Rome as his guest."

I nodded. "I can't disagree with either of you. He played his own son for a fool. I never thought he'd do that, but I can see now he has."

"Does it lead you," Lukas asked, "to question other things he's told you?"

"I suppose it should," I said. "But what do we do now?"

"Lukas and I," Timon replied, "propose doing nothing. We wish to counter your father's blatant dishonesty with blatant dishonesty of our own. We intend to act as if we see no connection whatsoever between our presence in Rome and his campaign for the consulship. We won't attend any of his speeches. We won't make any statement or take any action to indicate we care whether the next consul is Brutus or your father. Our purpose is to avoid a fight with your father."

"In the meantime," I asked, "you'll stay here in Rome?"

"We'll stay here in Rome," Lukas replied. "We'll sleep in your bed with you."

"We'll do that," Timon said, "as long as you don't say a word to your father we're perfectly aware of, and opposed to, what he's doing."

"I promise you," I said, "I won't say a word to my father about any of this. You know I'm in love with you guys."

"And you know," Lukas said, "we're in love with you."

"In the meantime," Timon said, "we've got other things we need to do. Lukas and I would like to go to Ostia this afternoon and swim in the sea. Can we ask Livia's warriors to take us there?"

"They'll gladly do it," I said. "They'll take turns swimming naked in the sea with us. They'll love it. They'll eat their evening meal with us. They've got a favorite place there, right on the beach. They'll love that too. My father will pay the bill. It won't cost them anything."

Timon

When we reached Ostia, I asked Livia to let me out of the carriage. I told her I'd walk the rest of the way to the sea. Marco and Lukas could begin swimming without me.

Livia chose to accompany me on foot. I decided she could've had two reasons for believing she was the only guard I needed. If her purpose was to protect me, she knew few people in Ostia would recognize me as long as I wasn't with Marco. If her purpose was to keep me from leaving Rome, she knew I'd never attempt to do it without Lukas.

"Would you mind," I asked her, "if I pay a visit to the market?"

"Not at all," she replied.

When we reached the market, I found the person I wished to speak with.

"She sells products from Greece," I told Livia.

"I know who she is," Livia said. "She and Thalia do a lot of business together."

I assumed Livia's position required her to know that.

In any event, Livia let me approach the vendor on my own and made no attempt to listen to our conversation, which was brief.

"Lukas and I," I said, "wish to see Thalia before her ship leaves Ostia."

"I'll let her know," the vendor said.

Thalia had assured Lukas and me the woman who sold Greek products in Ostia would do that.

I returned to Livia and laughed. "I'm ready to go swimming in the sea."

Marco

My father came home even later that evening than Timon, Lukas and I did. When I saw him, he said nothing about running for the consulship. Neither did I.

When I got up the next morning, I learned from Domenic and Philo he'd already left for the city.

Domenic laughed. "He's busy drumming up votes from the plebeians he despises."

Philo shook his head. "Many of them will vote for him without any drumming up from him. He captured a city and won a war. Not many people do that."

Timon

Lukas and I filled a basket with mushrooms we found in the woods west of the house. We didn't need to go past a guard post to enter and explore it. Marco carried the basket. He admitted he knew nothing about mushrooms.

When we gave them to Domenic and Philo, they removed them one at a time from the basket, and together passed judgment upon them.

"Not one of these will kill us," Philo said after they'd finished their inspection. "How did you know which to pick and which to leave where they grew?"

Lukas chose to answer that question. "Queen Helen's mother Leda was our instructor. She lived alone in a forest when she gave birth to Helen and her sister Clytemnestra. Her lover, a prince who later became the king, brought her every document he could find in the royal library with information about mushrooms. In that same library in Leda's childhood, she'd taught herself and the prince how to read."

Domenic turned to me and blinked. "So you're the descendant of two royal families. Both of your grandfathers were kings."

I shrugged. "For whatever it's worth, that's true. But I still think I'd be a plebeian in Rome."

Philo finished placing the mushrooms in the basket again.

"With some onions and cream," he said, "we'll make a soup."

He and Domenic included the soup in the midday meal Marco, Lukas and I ate with them in the dining room.

Chapter Twelve

Timon

Having consumed my first bowl of soup, I turned to Philo. "I don't understand why Marco's father thinks he can win the election. Isn't it true every plebeian eighteen and older can vote now, and they far outnumber the patricians?"

"You think," Philo asked, "the plebeians will all vote for the plebeian candidate, and the patricians will all vote for the patrician?"

"Won't they?" I asked.

Philo shook his head. "I very much doubt that's the way it will go. Most of the plebeians work for patricians and want to remain on good terms with their employers. Take this estate as an example. On election day Domenic and I and all the other workers here will gather in the village and vote. How many of the plebeians in that crowd do you think will vote for the senatorial candidate pledged to support Brutus?"

Domenic laughed. "Damned few. And those who do will probably later tell Old Marco they did it only because they were confused. After all, they'll say, it was the first time they voted."

"So why," I asked, "does Brutus think he can win the election?"

Philo once again gave me a condescending look. "Not all the patricians favor Old Marco. He has more than a few enemies among them. His warriors can sometimes be rather high-handed in their dealings with people, and he tends to let them get away with it. And some of the patricians favor Old Marco themselves, but they won't attempt to dictate how their workers vote. Some of them might simply choose not to be present when their workers vote."

"So the election is a tossup?" Lukas asked.

Philo nodded. "At this point, I'd say it is."

Marco

Thalia came to my father's house that afternoon to deliver some goods from Greece Domenic and Philo had ordered. She always brought them in a wagon pulled by two horses she drove herself.

Timon, Lukas and I helped her carry the items into the house.

When we were done, she said she'd like to speak with the three of us.

I suggested we sit on the benches on the balcony above the courtyard.

Thalia had learned my father was running for the consulship.

"Brutus," she said, "is using his opponent's great victory in the battle at Coriolis against him."

"I would've thought," I said, "my father's victory at Coriolis would be the main reason plebeians as well as patricians would vote for him."

Thalia looked at me and shook her head. "Brutus says it proves your father is out to destroy Rome's republican form of government."

My father said that was the lie Brutus told the Roman people every chance he got.

"And just how," I asked, "does my father's victory at Coriolis prove that?"

"Your father," Thalia replied, "began and fought that battle without any authorization from the senate or the consul—the people's senate and consul he'd sworn to serve."

"He was forced to do that," I said. "The Volscians were gathering their forces on the other side of the city. He couldn't wait any longer for the senators and consul to debate the issue. He couldn't sit idly while the Volscians captured the city. If he'd done that, it would've cost the Romans a dreadful amount of blood and treasure to take the city away from them."

Thalia scoffed. "Brutus says the Volscians and the Romans had both agreed not to invade Coriolis as long as the negotiations between them continued. Your father knew that too."

I nodded. "My father knew that. He also knew the Volscians

could and would break their agreement the moment their army reached its full strength on their side of the city."

"Brutus is telling the people," Thalia said, "that never would've happened. He says the Volscians knew how to count. They could see, even when their army reached its full strength, your father's warriors would still greatly outnumber theirs. Their negotiators privately admitted that to the Romans they were talking with."

"That doesn't make sense," I said. "If the Volscians knew they were outnumbered, why didn't they agree to remove their army from the border and let us have the city?"

"According to Brutus," Thalia said, "the Volscians were asking the Romans to let the people of Coriolis vote and decide for themselves whether they wanted to be a part of the Volscian kingdom or the Roman republic. Brutus says they would've voted for Rome. Almost all of them, he says, chose to stay in the city after your father captured it."

I admit I was confused at that point in my argument with Thalia. "Why didn't the senate and consul let my father know the Volscians wanted to put the matter to a vote of the people of Coriolis?"

"They did let him know," Thalia replied. "The senate and consul had kept him informed."

I shook my head. "My father never told me anything about a vote."

Lukas scoffed. "He also never told you anything about running for the consulship."

Thalia laughed and turned to me. "Your father, of course, doesn't believe in letting the people vote on anything. Brutus says he wasn't about to wait for a vote. Without any authorization from the consul or the senate, he decided to invade Coriolis. He chose to fight a battle his navy and army never needed to fight. Brutus says he did it for the glory. He wanted the people to think he, unlike the consul and the senate, was a Roman who could get things done."

I'd thought Thalia and my father were friends. They did so much business together. Her ships had brought to Rome many of the best arms his warriors fought with. They were far superior, they told me, to what they called the duck-hunting weapons Roman craftsmen made.

"Do you think," Timon asked Thalia, "Brutus's charges can make a difference in the election for the new senate?"

"I've heard they can," Thalia replied, "Old Marco's popularity rests upon his victory in the battle at Coriolis. If the people agree it was a battle as unnecessary as it was unauthorized, his chances of winning the consulship could go down the drain."

It was difficult for me to imagine my father losing an election to Brutus. Then again, it was even more difficult for me to imagine my father choosing to run against Brutus in an election. Thalia was right. My father didn't want the people voting on anything.

Thalia had kept her eyes on Timon. "There's something else you should know. Whenever Old Marco gives a speech, he reminds his audience you're his guest in Rome. He calls you Prince Timon of Troy. He doesn't come right out and say you endorse his candidacy for the consulship, but he does leave the impression you favor him."

Lukas turned to me. "What do you say about that? Would you agree Brutus was right when he told Timon your father was using him?"

It took me a moment before I could begin my response to those questions. "I won't argue with you about that. I just wish my father had told me he intended to run for the consulship during your visit here."

"Do you think," Thalia asked, "your father deliberately withheld that information from you?"

I shrugged. "He should've told me." I turned to Timon and Lukas. "I hope you believe me. I had no idea my father would run for the consulship while you were in Rome."

"I believe you," Lukas said, "but I think your father is a liar."

Timon nodded. "I agree with Lukas—on both points."

Chapter Thirteen

Timon

After Thalia left, Lukas and I remained on the balcony with Marco. The conversation seemed to have torn him apart. Every time he'd attempted to defend his father, Thalia had dismissed his arguments as if they were dead leaves in an autumn wind.

Lukas was no help. "To be honest," he said to Marco, "even if I were a Roman patrician, I'd never vote for your father."

Marco looked as if he were ready to shed tears. "I can't blame you for having an unfavorable opinion of my father at this point. He should've let us know he'd be running for the consulship now."

"He also should've let us know," Lukas said, "he intended to use his guest, Prince Timon of Troy, to drum up votes."

Marco nodded. "I agree."

Lukas wasn't done. "His failure to be honest with Prince Timon of Troy and his own son makes me strongly doubt he's been honest with the Roman people or will have any greater regard for the truth if he's the consul."

Marco made no attempt to respond to that thrust of the dagger.

Marco

We ate our evening meal again with Domenic and Philo. Neither they nor I knew where my father was.

All of us, even Lukas, chose to speak of other things, like the food we ate, Domenic's flowers in the courtyard and Philo's paintings on the walls.

After we finished our supper, Lukas and Timon ascended the stairs to the second floor. When we reached the door to my bedroom, I turned to them.

"I don't suppose," I said, "you still have any interest in spending the night in my bed."

Lukas chose to embrace me. "Why wouldn't we?" he asked. "You're not your father. You're not to blame for what he's doing. I'll be damned if I'll let that man come between you and us."

"That's right," Timon said, embracing me as soon as Lukas let go of me. "Lukas and I were warned not to come here. Thalia warned us. So did my mother and Menelaus. We didn't pay any attention to them. Just like you, our minds were focused on something else."

"What was the something else?" I asked.

Lukas smirked. "The three of us getting into bed together."

He pushed me through the doorway and followed me into my room.

"And right now," he said, "I want to see the three of us getting into your bed together."

Lukas had neither my height nor girth, but I never would've challenged either him or Timon to a fight, even if I'd been deranged enough to think I had a reason to.

Marco

The next morning Timon, Lukas and I ate raisins and dates on the balcony above the courtyard.

My father had come home again the previous night after we'd gone to bed. He'd left this morning before we got up. I wondered if he didn't want any confrontations with the guests he'd invited to Rome under false pretenses.

During our talk with Thalia the previous afternoon, I was certain Timon and Lukas had decided I was a hopeless fool they no longer needed in their lives. After we returned to my bed that night, though, they made it seem as if nothing at all had come between us.

Timon looked at me. "We're prisoners here."

"What makes you think that?" I asked.

Who Killed Coriolanus?

"Your father," Timon said, "has this house surrounded. If we tried to leave here, it wouldn't matter which direction we took. The warriors in your father's guard posts would see us and go with us wherever we went. If we reached Ostia and tried to board a ship bound for Greece, they'd stop us."

"They might stop me," I said "But what makes you think they'd stop you and Lukas? I've never heard they're supposed to keep the two of you from leaving Rome."

"You haven't heard a lot of things," Lukas said. "Your father wouldn't want Timon and me leaving Rome during his election campaign. And he can keep us from doing it. We're all his prisoners here."

Marco

"We might be able to get past the guard posts," I said, having emptied my bowl of raisins and dates. "I did it once. It wasn't easy, but I did it."

Timon and Lukas looked at me as if I'd told them I knew where a hoard of gold was hidden.

"The guards didn't see you?" Lukas asked.

For some reason he decided I needed his arm around my shoulders. I didn't need it, but I liked it there anyway.

"They didn't see me," I said. "I walked all the way to the coast and back. Nobody saw me."

"How did you do it?" Timon asked. "You've got to show us how you did it."

I nodded toward the west. "See how that rocky hill rises up on the other side of the woods? Not far from where you picked those mushrooms, there's an opening in the rocks where they begin to slope upward. It's behind some evergreen bushes. You could walk by it a thousand times and never know it was there. But it's actually an entrance to a cave under the hill."

"Tell us more," Lukas said.

"A few years ago," I said, "I was in the woods on a summer day looking for a place I could take my clothes off and, you know, relieve my tension. I saw a rabbit, and just for the hell of it, I followed it behind the bushes. It jumped into the opening, and I decided to go where it did."

"That was the entrance to the cave?" Lukas asked, tightening his arm around my shoulders, whispering his question in my ear.

No wonder, I thought, Timon was in love with him.

"It was," I replied.

"Where did the rabbit take you?" Timon asked.

"To the western end of the cave. I could walk upright for a while. Eventually, though, I had to get down on my hands and knees to go where the rabbit went."

Lukas shook me a bit, as if I'd fallen asleep.

I'd merely closed my eyes because it felt so good to have him and Timon on either side of me whispering in my ears.

"At the western end of the cave," I continued, "there's a much smaller opening than the one in the woods. It's a mere slit in the rocks. I could get through it, though. It was hidden like the entrance, behind another patch of evergreen bushes. After I got out of the cave, I knew damned well I was beyond the guard posts. I knew where the two closest were. I also knew I was well beyond where the warriors at those posts could see me."

"You kept going?" Lukas asked.

"I did," I replied. "It was like I was in a different world. My father had warned me never to go anywhere unless his warriors were with me. Too many people out there would like to abduct me, maybe even kill me. I was his son. That's what a lot of people in Rome would do to his son."

"But you kept going anyway?" Lukas asked.

I nodded. "I walked all the way to the sea."

"Nobody saw you?" Timon ask.

"Nobody saw me," I said. "I found a secluded cove. It's south of Ostia. Nobody was in or near it. I'd never heard anybody mention it before."

"So what did you do then?" Lukas asked.

"I took off my clothes," I said. "I sat in the afternoon sun."

"You relieved your tension?" Lukas asked.

I nodded again. "That's what I did. After I finished, I fell asleep. When I woke up again, I put my clothes on, came back to the cave, crawled through it and came home."

Marco

"Did you tell anybody what you'd done?" Timon asked.

I shook my head. "Nobody. Never. Not until now."

"Not even Domenic and Philo?" Lukas asked.

"No," I replied, "definitely not them."

"Why *definitely not them?*" Lukas asked.

"They would've told my father I'd disobeyed him," I said. "They're as strict as he is about where I go. They're loyal to him. They've lived all their lives with him. He got them out of Troy at the last moment, when it was in flames. Ever since, they've told me, they've wanted his protection more than anything else. They say they have a good deal here. My father lets them do whatever they want. They choose the food they prepare and the four of us eat. They decorate the walls. They grow the flowers."

I had to pause to fight back my tears.

"Domenic and Philo raised me," I said, "as if they were my parents. My only real parent, my father, spent most of his days with his warriors and sailors. Domenic and Philo took care of me. They taught me reading and writing and everything else a patrician is supposed to know. But they never let me forget their safety and mine depended upon one strong person guiding us, deciding for us what to do."

Lukas and Timon had their arms entwined around my shoulders like vines.

"Was Helen," I asked them, "the one strong person guiding

you?"

"She was," Timon replied.

"She didn't do it, though," Lukas said, "with armed warriors."

Timon

Domenic and Philo filled our knapsacks with food for our lunch.

Marco told Lukas and me we couldn't let them know we intended to eat the food in a secluded cove with a rocky cliff at our backs and a view of the sea in front of us. They'd be certain to ask how many warriors were going with us. Our guardians would also need food for their lunch. And whose would they appreciate more than Domenic and Philo's?

Marco easily found the evergreen bushes hiding the entrance to the cave. Lukas and I remembered seeing them when we'd searched the woods for mushrooms.

Reaching the western end of the cave, we discovered we had to do some digging. Marco wasn't fully grown when he'd crawled through it on his hands and knees.

We took turns digging. The two of us taking a break from the hard work pushed the soil between our haunches back to the more spacious part of the cave.

After we crawled through the narrow exit, we agreed we'd have no need to do any pushups or sit-ups that day.

Marco looked in every direction. "I know we're beyond my father's warriors. They can't see us here. I've spent lots of time at all their posts, you know."

Lukas laughed. "Looking them over to decide which of them you'd invite to share your bed?"

Marco seemed a bit rueful. "Only one of them ever did that."

"Was he," I asked, "the only one you ever invited to do that?"

Marco nodded. "He was."

Chapter Fourteen

Timon

Marco led us over rocky wastelands and through dark woods to avoid coming into contact with any of his father's workers. He said they'd all recognize him, and most of them would report they'd seen him at a great distance from the house without any armed warriors protecting him.

"My father," Marco said, trudging forward, "would make me tell him how I'd sneaked away from my guards."

"How would he make you do that?" Lukas asked.

"He has warriors," Marco replied, "who know how to persuade a person to cough up information. They create pain and cleverly increase it without causing permanent injuries. If he had to, my father would hand me over to those people."

Lukas couldn't conceal his struggle to make sense of what he'd heard. "Your father would torture his own son?"

Marco grimaced. "I'd never let it go that far. My father doesn't tolerate disobedience. He's personally executed warriors guilty of nothing more than petty theft. He says disobedient warriors are worthless warriors."

Marco

I led Timon and Lukas down the cliff to the cove. We had it all to ourselves.

We washed the clothes we'd dirtied in the cave and hung them on rocks to dry in the afternoon sun and breeze. We ate every morsel of the food Domenic and Philo had placed in our knapsacks, not knowing how hungry we'd be when we ate it, or why.

We hadn't nearly as much time as we would've liked, though, for what we most wanted to do in the cove that afternoon.

We had to return to the house for supper. Domenic and Philo would wonder how we'd spent the whole day in the woods without capturing the duck they'd asked us to bring home.

I knew what Domenic would say, shaking his head as if he'd witnessed the end of the world. "Three young men as fit as they can be, and not a single duck among them to roast."

Home again, though, I handed him the unlucky fowl Lukas had caught as he hit the water after jumping off a ledge above the pond in the woods.

"No wonder," Philo said, admiring the way Lukas's tunic clung to his body, "you're soaked."

"I can only imagine," Domenic said, "this duck didn't see you coming."

Lukas laughed. "I'd be awfully embarrassed if a duck saw me coming."

But he hadn't seemed at all shy earlier in the afternoon when at least a dozen seagulls saw him doing that in the cove.

Marco

I crossed paths with my father later that evening. I asked him how his campaign for the consulship was going.

He shrugged. "We have a lot of stupid people in this world with us."

We were in the hallway between our rooms. I'd forced myself to stay awake after Timon and Lukas had fallen asleep. I wanted to hear my father arriving home.

"I thought Romans," I said, "were a bright people, even as bright as the Greeks."

"They could be if they put to good use the brains they were born with."

"Too many of them believe what Brutus tells them?"

My father nodded, with an audible sigh. "And it's so damned

easy to see through the lies he tells."

Apparently, though, the people weren't required to see through the lies the commander of their army and navy told them.

Timon

The next afternoon Lukas and I walked to the village with Marco. Because we'd proved, the day before, we had nothing better to do, Domenic and Philo asked us to go to the market with their hand wagon and bring home a number of items they needed for their pantry.

Marco told us the merchants and the other buyers in the market would be amused when they saw what we were doing.

"What will amuse them?" Lukas asked.

"Only Domenic and Philo," Marco replied, "can ask a patrician's son to go to the village and pick up items they need for their pantry. Servants are supposed to do that themselves. But this day will be especially unusual. The patrician's son will have Prince Timon of Troy and his Spartan companion with him to help carry the groceries home."

When the armed guards joined us on our way to the village, I struck up a conversation with Livia.

I had a few questions for her. "Do warriors accompany Marco's father when he goes to the city asking the people to vote for him?"

She laughed and shook her head. "The commander of the Roman army and navy says he doesn't need protection. He'd recognize any danger to himself as soon as he saw it, and he'd do whatever he needed to do to make it go away."

"But his youthful son," I said, "might not recognize danger to himself and do what he needed to do?"

Livia glanced at Marco, who walked ahead of us with Lukas pulling Domenic and Philo's wagon. "That's what his father fears the most."

"Does his father at least let his army know where he is and what he's doing?"

Livia shook her head again. "We know where he is and what he's doing only when he's at the base. Otherwise, he could be sailing on a ship in the sea with the navy, tending to political matters in the city, or doing who knows what anywhere else he might please to be. He says a well-trained army has no need to remain in constant contact with its commander. His deputies know exactly what to do during any imaginable situation arising during his absence."

Marco had told us Livia was one of those deputies.

"We've learned," she continued, "where Old Marco's gone and what he's been doing in the past several days since he announced he was running for consul."

"Giving speeches to the people," I asked, "plebeians as well as patricians?"

Livia nodded.

I had another question. "Do you and your comrades in the army and navy believe he'll win the election?"

Livia waited a moment before she responded to that one.

"I'd guess," she said, "most of my comrades doubt he'll win."

"Even though he won the battle at Coriolis?"

"The people loved him for that. But he was only the commander of the army and navy then. If he becomes the consul with the backing of a majority of the senators, he'll control the prices the people have to pay for grain. I suspect the wish of the plebeians for lower grain prices will outweigh any admiration they might have for Old Marco's decisive victory at Coriolis."

"Did you fight there?"

"I was in the bow of the first Roman ship to enter the harbor. I fired arrows at the sailors on the ships defending the city. My companion is an excellent shield-holder. Neither of us suffered a significant injury from their archers."

"Was she your shield-holder in Troy?"

Livia frowned. "My companion in Troy died the same day your father died. On the same rooftop too."

Livia and I turned to one another.

"I'm very sorry to hear that," I said.

"Achilles died that day as well," Livia said. "But it was also the day we Trojans realized we could fight no longer."

Livia and I walked for a bit in silence.

I broke it with yet another question. "You killed enemy combatants in the battle for Coriolis?"

"My arrows struck a number of them. I learned later some of them suffered fatal wounds."

"And you and your companion in Troy knew my father and mother?"

"We knew them well. More than a few times, we held you in our arms."

Marco

Domenic and Philo had asked us to buy dates and other imported goods from a merchant who was an outspoken supporter of Brutus. Her political opinions never seemed to hurt her business in the village. Even my father knew Domenic and Philo bought items from her, but he made no attempt to stop them.

"Only two things matter," he told me after I'd asked him about it. "Her goods are among the best the shippers bring to Rome, and her prices for them, compared to what the other sellers are charging, are better. Her misguided thoughts on Brutus and the Roman government are irrelevant."

"I hope," she said, as I gave her the silver I'd agreed to pay her, "your father is prepared for his defeat on election day. Too many of the best workers have dared their employers to fire them if they vote for Brutus. Too many patricians have given in to their workers and told them they can vote for anybody they please."

As she so often did, the merchant spoke loudly enough to attract the attention of anybody who happened to be nearby.

One of my older guards, who spoke his mind as freely as the merchant did, chose to respond. "The plebeians can cast all their votes for Brutus on election day, but that doesn't mean their hero will be the next consul. It will mean, instead, this will be the last election day Rome will see."

Timon and Lukas turned to me.

"*The last election day Rome will see?*" Lukas asked, speaking so softly only Timon, the merchant and I could hear him. "What does he mean by that?"

"He means," the merchant undertook to answer the question for me, "despite the vote against him, Old Marco will declare himself the consul and do away with future elections."

"Will he abolish the senate too?" Lukas asked.

The merchant nodded. "I'm afraid many of his warriors and sailors want him to do that."

I should've seen this coming. I'd made no mention of the possibility of a republic-abolishing scenario to my guests from peace-loving Sparta. I'd heard what the merchant had heard, but I'd never believed my father would actually name himself consul and destroy the republic.

Chapter Fifteen

Timon

During our walk home from the village, Livia and I spoke privately again.

"Did you hear," I asked, "your comrade tell us Old Marco might lose the election to Brutus but claim the consulship for himself anyway?"

Livia nodded. "I heard what he said."

"Do you believe the army and navy would support Old Marco if he did that?"

"I believe they would. All the warriors and sailors under his command owe their positions to him and him alone. Their loyalty is to him—not to a form of government. Your presence in Rome at this moment reminds every Roman of one thing."

"What's that?"

"A republic run by popularly elected senators and a consul the senators elect isn't a necessity in this world. And when the senators and the consul squabble over every little decision they make, they don't help the argument for their continued existence."

"And yet a single, unaccountable ruler, a Hector, can make the tragic mistake he made."

"The people have put Hector out of their minds. They remember your father and mother and the difference they came so close to making. They could've saved magnificent, beautiful, bountiful Troy and its people."

I wanted to contend that proved my point, but instead I made no response.

"You should know something else," Livia said.

I felt I'd been as open to learning lately as a flower to the bees.

"What else should I know?" I asked.

"I tried to save your father's life, but I failed."

She and I turned to one another and paused, letting the others in our party pass us by.

"Please," I said, "I beg you, tell me how that happened."

"I saw your father aim his arrow at Achilles. I saw the Greek archer aim her arrow at your father. I aimed my arrow at her. When your father shot his arrow, I shot mine at the Greek archer. Her shield holder had her covered too well, though. I couldn't hit the archer, but I could hit her shield, and I did. I thought the force of my arrow striking her shield might jar her shield holder and herself just enough to cause her arrow to miss your father. But they were too strong and steady. My arrow might as well have been a butterfly landing on the Greek archer's shield. I'm very sorry I couldn't save your father's life. Then, in the commotion on our rooftop after your father's death, my shield holder became exposed. The Greek archer who'd killed your father shot another arrow and killed my companion."

Livia and I had no more words to exchange. As if she were my mother and I her son, we embraced.

Marco

After Timon, Lukas and I carried the goods on the hand wagon into Domenic and Philo's pantry, Timon and Lukas climbed the stairs to the balcony. Once again, they didn't ask me to join them.

Even from the other end of the courtyard, where I sat on a bench drinking from my cup of wine, I could tell they were as alarmed as I was. And I felt certain their apprehension and mine had arisen from the same source—the loud talk in the village of what my father might do if he lost the election for the consulship.

After Timon and Lukas spoke privately as long as they needed to, they came down from the balcony and joined me on my bench.

Timon went straight to the heart of the matter. "Lukas and I have decided to leave Rome as soon as we can."

Who Killed Coriolanus?

Marco

"Why do you wish to leave Rome," I asked, even as I knew they saw nothing but trouble ahead in Rome.

"Your people," Timon replied, "are on the verge of a civil war."

Lukas nodded. "And we want no part in it. We'd much rather be in Sparta while your Romans kill one another."

"A civil war?" I asked. "Romans killing one another? I'm afraid I don't understand what you're talking about."

"Your father," Timon said, "is about to lose the election for the consulship. And he'll lose to his archenemy Brutus. Then your father, despite losing the election, will appoint himself the consul. His army and navy will support him. Brutus and his followers, though, will never go along with the abolition of the republic. It's their only hope to have any say in running the country. They'll never give it up."

"A civil war?" I asked again. "Romans killing one another?"

"Your father's army and navy," Timon said, "will face off against the plebeians."

"Brutus's plebeians," Lukas said, "will vastly outnumber your father's warriors and sailors. But the army and navy will have vastly superior weaponry and training. Many of their weapons came from Greece. The plebeians will only have a few hunting bows and arrows, but they'll have more than enough pitchforks, axes and butcher knives for every one of them to wield. Even the old people and children will have weapons."

"You'll end up in a bloody civil war," Timon said. "It could go on forever."

"And we want nothing to do with it," Lukas said. "That's why we intend to leave Rome as soon as we can."

"When do you think that will be?" I asked.

"After Thalia's ship returns," Lukas replied.

"When will that be?" I asked.

"She told us," Timon said, "she planned to return to Rome the day after the election."

"We'll use the escape route you found," Lukas said. "If your father's warriors catch us attempting to leave, we're certain they'll bring us back here, to our prison. So we'll sneak around them through the cave."

I threw my arms around Lukas and Timon both. "I don't want to lose you," I said. "You know I'm in love with you."

"You're more than welcome," Lukas said, "to come with us to Sparta."

"We'd prefer," Timon said, "you come with us to Sparta. You'll be safe there from your father's enemies."

"You want me to leave my father?" I asked. "You want me to leave Domenic and Philo? You want me to leave the people I've lived all my life with?"

"We do want you to do that," Lukas said. "It'll be the best way to keep you alive."

"And with us," Timon said.

Timon

At supper that evening, Lukas asked Domenic and Philo if they'd heard any talk of Old Marco ignoring the results of the election and naming himself the consul.

"His warriors and sailors want him to do that," Philo replied.

"All of them?" I asked.

"Most of them," Philo said.

Domenic nodded. "All those who've been with him the longest do. They understand a republic is no way to run a country."

"Do you agree with them?" Lukas asked.

Domenic laughed. "Anybody in their right mind would agree with them."

I looked at Philo. "Do you agree with them?"

He shrugged. "Brutus appeals to the worst instincts of

uneducated people. I think he's proved what's wrong with letting all the people decide who their leaders should be."

Despite being servants and plebeians, Domenic and Philo had been Marco's tutors. Lukas and I had seen and admired the extensive library Philo had put together in a large second-story room. Many of the documents in it were written in Greek.

Unlike Philo and Domenic, the tutors of other patrician children were patricians, usually after they'd completed their service in the army or navy. The best of them, Philo had told us, borrowed documents from his library.

"But won't the plebeians resist?" I asked. "They just gained the right to vote in the elections. After electing one of their own to the consulship, surely they won't let Old Marco abolish the republic."

"They can resist all they want," Domenic said. "Old Marco will have the warriors and sailors behind him."

"But the plebeians," Lukas said, "will vastly outnumber the warriors and sailors. They got what they wanted in their grain riots."

"They got what they wanted," Domenic said, "only because the consul and senators wouldn't use the warriors and sailors against them. Old Marco wanted to kill as many of the plebeians as it took to stop the riots. But the cowardly consul and senators refused to let him do it."

Marco seemed surprised. "My father wanted to end the riots by killing plebeians?"

"As many of them as it took," Domenic replied.

Lukas turned to Marco. "You didn't know that?"

"We do our best," Philo said, "to protect Marco from that sort of news."

I stared across the table at Philo. "Protect him? How does keeping Marco in the dark on something as momentous as killing a large number of plebeians protect him?"

Domenic laughed. "Welcome to Rome."

He laughed alone.

Lukas turned to Philo. "Does Marco's father want you to protect his son from the big, bad world he lives in?"

"Marco's father," Philo replied, "is the person Domenic and I work for. It's always been that way."

"All the way back to Troy?" I asked.

Philo nodded. "That far back—a long way back."

Chapter Sixteen

Marco

Timon and Lukas had become as loving toward me as I'd dreamed they'd be. But every day since our landing in Rome had brought developments making me regret I'd talked them into leaving Sparta and becoming guests in my father's house.

"Your father isn't protecting you," Lukas said when we reached my bedroom that night. "He's protecting himself."

"How's he protecting himself?" I asked.

Lukas glowered. "He's attempting to keep you from becoming an adult with a mind of your own. He's very afraid of that. And he should be."

"What do you mean?" I asked. "Why should my father be afraid of me?"

"Parents like your father," Lukas said, "should be afraid any children of theirs will grow up and come to understand they should turn on them."

Nobody could fault Lukas for failing to speak his mind.

"Go to Philo's library," he said. "The documents in it, or any library worth visiting, are filled with their stories."

I'd read many of those stories, but I'd never seen myself in them. I wondered now if it was a matter of not wanting to.

Timon

Marco, Lukas and I ran the next morning from one guard post to the next surrounding the house. Marco had agreed Lukas and I should know the contours of the prison we'd found ourselves in.

When we reached Livia's post for the second time, Marco and Lukas ran back to the house without me. I stopped to speak with Livia.

She and I sat alone on a bench on the flat top of the hill the post occupied. We could look in one direction and see the house. We could look in the opposite direction and see the village.

The youngest, and therefore lowest-ranking, warrior she commanded brought both of us a large bowl of salad for our midday meal. Livia told me the warrior had gotten the recipe for the tiny spring greens with olive oil and crumbled goat cheese from Domenic and Philo.

Was this the warrior, I wondered, who'd shared Marco's bed? Was that why Domenic and Philo had given him their recipe?

I turned to Livia. "I'm curious to know one thing, just to be prepared. When will Old Marco declare himself the new consul—if, of course, that's what he intends to do. Will he make the announcement as soon as the results of the election are in?"

Livia shook her head. "I doubt he'll do it then. He'll wait until the plebeians in the city have finished celebrating their great victory and gone back to work. He won't need to make the announcement until the new senate is prepared to elect Brutus. One of Old Marco's justifications for claiming the consulship for himself and abolishing the republic will be to keep a plebeian from ever holding the office."

"How soon after the election will that be?"

"Three or four days."

I thought about that for a few moments. I wanted Lukas and me to be gone from Rome before it happened.

"The plebeians," I said, "seem to know what Old Marco intends to do."

Livia nodded. "I've been told many of them are aware of the threat."

"What would happen if one of the plebeians, or a gang of them, killed Old Marco before he declared himself consul?"

Livia frowned.

"You told me," I said, "he's been riding in his chariot to the city and back every day alone. A well-led gang of plebeians could assassinate him. If they were clever enough, they could even get away with it."

Livia nodded again. "That concerns many of his supporters in the army and navy. I hear them talking about it."

"If the plebeians murdered Old Marco, would one of his supporters claim the consulship?"

Livia shook her head. "I can't imagine any of them doing that. Old Marco has taken all the credit for the capture of Coriolis. He's been the commander of the army and navy since the first days of Rome. Nobody else could get away with the abolition of the republic. He might be able to do it, though. I doubt a single warrior or sailor will refuse to obey his commands."

Timon

On election-day morning Domenic, Philo and Marco walked to the village to vote. Lukas and I went with them. After we reached Livia's guard post, a warrior accompanied each of us the rest of the way to the village. Livia chose to be my guard.

The voting took place in the market. Buying and selling during the voting was prohibited.

Domenic, Philo and Marco joined the inhabitants of the village on one side of the market. The two election officials—the caller and the counter—stood on the other side. Lukas and I remained with the warriors at the entrance to the market.

"I thought," I said to Livia, in a low voice only she and Lukas could hear, "Old Marco would wish to be present, to make certain his workers vote for him."

She laughed. "He doesn't need to be here personally to accomplish that. One of the warriors guarding you—I can't tell you which one—is observing the vote for him. Two of his long-term workers will also let him know who votes for whom."

I didn't want to put Livia on the spot by asking her if the observers she'd referred to were herself, Domenic and Philo.

The caller began the proceeding. "This is the first call," she said,

95

her voice deep, loud and commanding, "for all those who wish to vote for one of the two candidates for senator from this constituency."

All the voters who wished to vote that day must've already been present. Nobody joined the crowd after the first call.

Moments later, the caller announced the second call for all those who wished to vote. Again, nobody came running to join the assembled voters.

Moments after that, the caller gave voice to the third and final call and, permitting no further delay, began the voting.

"All those," she said, "who wish to vote for the candidate pledged to Brutus step forward now."

Seven merchants, including the woman who sold dates and other imported goods, stepped forward.

The counter went from voter to voter pointing at them as he counted.

Then he turned to the caller. "Seven votes for the candidate pledged to Brutus."

"All those," the caller said, "who wish to vote for the candidate pledged to Coriolanus step forward now."

All the remaining voters, with one exception, stepped forward.

Again, the counter went from voter to voter, pointing and counting.

The one voter who'd conspicuously abstained was Marco.

"Do you know why," Livia asked Lukas and me, "Marco isn't voting?"

"He told us this morning," Lukas replied, "he thought it would be unseemly for him to vote for or against his father. He decided to come here to make public his abstention,"

I wondered—but, once again, chose not to ask—if Livia would include that explanation in her report to Old Marco.

Chapter Seventeen

Marco

Timon, Lukas and I walked back to the village late that same afternoon. Domenic and Philo had told us they'd have supper ready for us when we returned.

As soon as we reached the market, I could tell my father had lost the election. As if we'd wandered onto a stage in the last act of a tragedy, I saw fear on every face in sight.

The merchant who sold dates approached me.

"For your sake," she said, "I'm sorry."

"Was the election close?" Timon asked.

"Not at all," the merchant replied. "More than two-thirds of the senators elected are pledged to Brutus."

Lukas turned to me. "Won't your father consider this a humiliation?"

"No," the loudmouthed guard said before I had a chance to reply. "He won't pay any attention to it. He'll be our next consul. I hope his first order rids Rome, one way or the other, of Brutus. We've had enough of him and his gang."

"And then," the merchant said, "you'll be fighting a war. Is that what you want?"

This time I answered the question before my guard had a chance to. "The last thing anybody in their right mind should want is a war."

Timon

When we returned to the house, Domenic and Philo told Marco his father had come home and wished to speak with all of us in the court-yard. They'd agreed we could eat supper after the conclusion of our discussion.

"Does he know," Marco asked, "he's lost the election by a large margin?"

Domenic and Philo both looked as if Marco had asked about a calamity in which an unthinkable number of people had perished.

"He knows," Philo replied.

Marco

My father had arranged three wooden benches in a triangle in the courtyard. He sat down on one and pointed his finger at another.

"You," he said, looking at me, "can sit there with Prince Timon of Troy and his companion."

I sat where my father told me to sit. Lukas and Timon sat on either side of me.

My father gestured toward Domenic and Philo to sit on the third bench.

I turned to my father. "So what will you do now? We went to the village and learned Brutus has won the election. More than two-thirds of the new senate will vote for him to be the consul of Rome."

"What happened today," my father replied, "doesn't concern me in the least."

"Why do you say that?" I asked. "You've told us, more than once, Brutus is totally unfit to be the consul of Rome. Do you now agree with the overwhelming majority of Romans whose votes shout loud and clear they believe he's more fit than you for the office?"

My father laughed as if I were a child whose insolence a wise parent pays no more attention to than a wise gardener does a close-flying bee.

"Elections," he replied, "like senators and consuls, have absolutely no place in a kingdom."

I could hear Timon and Lukas gasp. Domenic and Philo sat stony-faced, as if my father's remark hadn't changed everything for all of us.

"You don't intend," I asked, "to declare yourself consul of

Rome?"

"I'd never do that," my father said. "The last thing I'd ever wish to be is a traitor."

I glanced at Timon. I turned my head one hundred and eighty degrees and glanced at Lukas. They knew, as I did, what was coming.

The light-hearted comedy I'd hoped their visit to Rome would be had become instead a dark tragedy. Each of the characters in my father's courtyard that afternoon was riding a chariot behind a runaway horse.

"So," I asked my father, "what do you intend to do now?"

"I don't intend to do anything at all," he replied. "The man seated to your left will make the next move."

Timon was seated to my left.

"Could you please describe for me," he asked my father, as if he didn't already know, "what that move will be?"

"You don't ask me," my father said, "what you'll do. I'm only the commander of your army and navy. You order me to do whatever it is you wish me to do."

"You want Timon," I asked my father, "to break the promise he made to the people of Rome when he visited the city and spoke with Brutus? You want Timon to do what he said he wouldn't do? You want him to claim his right to rule Rome as its king?"

"That's precisely," my father replied, "what I imagine he will do, whether I want him to do it or not. A king can always change his mind."

"But suppose," Timon said, "I did change my mind. I'd be a hapless king. I know so little about this country and its people. How could I hand down thoughtful orders? How could I render reasonable decisions in the controversies the people would ask me to hear?"

My father looked at Timon as he so often did me, as if I'd always be an innocent boy who'd need to be told what to do.

"You have nothing to worry about," my father said. "You'll hand down my thoughtful orders. You won't have to waste your time hearing the crybaby people yourself. My most trustworthy warriors will do that. They'll honestly report to me the facts of each and every case. I'll carefully study those facts and render your reasonable decisions."

"You want Timon to be a figurehead king," I said. "You'll have all the powers he or any king should have."

My father, staring at Timon, ignored me.

"Ruling Rome," he said, "will be easy for you. Except for a few special occasions every year, you won't need to go to the city and appear before the people. You'll have little contact with them. My warriors won't let them come near you. You'll live in this well-protected house with my son, your companion and my two servants. You'll have nothing more to worry about when you rise from your bed every morning than what you'll do with them that day to entertain yourself. You'll live the life befitting a king of Troy or Rome. All the burdens of your kingship will fall where they should—on me, the loyal commander of your army and navy."

I decided I'd attempt once more to gain my father's attention. "What if Timon declines to claim his lawful right to be the king of Rome? What if he decides instead to abdicate and grant all his powers to the senate and consul of Rome?"

My father once again kept his eyes on Timon, but he did choose to answer my questions.

"I doubt," he said, "Timon would wish to do that. He knows by now, I'm certain, my warriors surround this house for his protection as well as yours. Those warriors are the best warriors any commander or king could ask for. But they do, as all mortals must, sometimes cause accidents to happen. I doubt Timon would wish to take any chance at all such a regretful accident could take the life of the beautiful Spartan youth he's brought with him to Rome."

I had to admit I was still an innocent child. I hadn't imagined my father would go so far. I never should've pleaded with Timon and Lukas to come to Rome with me. I should've realized I was asking them to join me in my prison.

Who Killed Coriolanus?

"Domenic and Philo tell me," my father said, again without taking his eyes off the sole remaining member of the Trojan royal family, "Timon is in love with Lukas as much as his father Paris was with his mother Helen. Domenic and Philo also tell me you're that much in love with both Timon and Lukas. Surely, you don't want to see any harm come to either of them."

Timon turned to me. "Don't worry yourself any further. I should claim my lawful right to rule Rome as its king. And I should grant your father the right to exercise my powers. He knows better than anybody else how to rule this country. You and Lukas and I shouldn't have to bother ourselves with the government of Rome. Your father and his warriors can do that for us. We should only have to decide how to enjoy our days together in this idyllic setting."

My father nodded. "Those are the kingly powers you'll keep for yourself and share, as you wish, with my son and your companion."

My father had correctly calculated his threat to murder Lukas would win Timon's unlikely assent to his plot to restore the Trojan monarchy in Rome, but with its commander of the army and navy running the show behind the scenes. I turned to Timon. I couldn't blame him. He had every reason to believe my father could and would follow through on his threat—and cast our lives into the darkness of the grave we'd dig for Lukas.

Timon

"One further thing," Old Marco said after we'd taken our usual places at the supper table, "I want none of you to speak to any other person of our plans for the government of Rome. Nobody else needs to know about them until three days from today."

"Why is that?" I asked. "Is that the day I'll claim my right to be the king of Rome and abolish the senate and the consulship?"

Old Marco nodded. "That will be the day you'll do it."

"The day before the new senate meets?"

101

Old Marco nodded again. "That day. And if Brutus and his supporters actually meet the next day, they'll prove what traitors they are."

"And need to be arrested?" Lukas asked.

Old Marco laughed. "Arrested, tried, sentenced to die and executed—all of them, together, as a group."

"Your warriors," I asked, "will handle all those things?"

"They will. You won't have to worry about any of it."

Even though all of it would be done in my name. The mad King Timon of Rome would order the arrests of the republican traitors, find them guilty of treason and sentence them to die. Considering the gravity of the occasion, I wondered if Old Marco would at least expect me to put in an appearance for their executions.

Chapter Eighteen

Timon

Old Marco had some advice for me as we finished eating dessert. "Don't ever forget, the people love you. You're the son of Paris and Helen. Now you've proved you're alive and well. You've come here because you care about the survivors of Troy and their descendants. The people have had enough of this foolish republic. You'll rescue them from it. They'll be very pleased to have a king again."

But surely not, I thought, a king who'd live idly with his companions and let the despised commander of the army and navy rule the country in his name.

"The people will never love *me*," Old Marco said, his voice whining as if he were reliving an especially vexing day in his childhood. "No, I maintain order in this land. I can only hope to earn *hatred* for what *I* do. It's like a mathematical equation. Greater order among the people equals greater hatred for the person imposing it."

Menelaus and my mother, on the other hand, maintained excellent order in their country and earned nothing but love for what they did.

Marco turned to his father. "Why do you wish to wait three days? Why can't Timon claim his right to be the king of Rome tomorrow?"

Old Marco shook his head. "I need to reinforce the guard posts surrounding this house. Timon will rule Rome from here. I'll need more of my warriors at each of the posts. The relocation I have in mind can't be done overnight. But I can expect my warriors to complete the job within the next two days."

I turned to Marco. "We'll require a lot more protection here. The supporters of Brutus will come for me, knowing my death will bring an end to the monarchy. I think your father has made a wise decision."

Marco

After supper that evening Timon and Lukas asked me to walk with them in the twilight as far as the woods. When we reached our destination, we remained standing under the outer edge of the trees.

"We wanted to make damned sure," Lukas said to me, "your father, Domenic and Philo couldn't hear what we need to say."

Timon nodded. "Your father had this planned all along. Using me as a figurehead king is the reason he sent you to Sparta to get me here. He invited Lukas to come with me to obtain the hostage he figured he might need."

"You can blame me," I said, "all you want. I got you into this. My father played me for the fool he knew I was—and I've proved to be. My only defense is, I never thought he'd go so far as to threaten either of you with harm, to say nothing of death."

Timon and Lukas had both begun shaking their heads as soon as they heard me say, "You can blame me."

"We aren't blaming you for anything," Timon said. "You were only doing what your father asked you to do."

"My father," I said, "has changed our lives forever. We'll have to be extremely cautious living here. I don't doubt my father will carry through on his threat to kill Lukas if you force him to. He's killed a large number of people in his life, and I know damned well he doesn't regret doing it. Whenever he's talked with me about killing people, he's seemed as proud as an athlete wearing a laurel wreath."

Timon frowned. "Lukas and I aren't going to stay here and let your father rule Rome in my name. That's going to lead to bloodshed and war. And Lukas and I don't want anything to do with it. We're getting out of here, Your father intends to let the people know I'm claiming the kingship of Rome three days from now, but we'll be gone by then. We and you will use the time between now and then to plan and execute our escape from your father's prison."

"I'll gladly help you and Lukas escape," I said.

Lukas shook his head again. "You'll have to escape too. You'll have to come with us to Sparta."

Who Killed Coriolanus?

"I'll have to go with you to Sparta?" I asked. "What are you talking about?"

"We can't escape from here," Lukas said, "unless you come with us. You don't have a choice."

"I don't have a choice?" I asked. "You expect me to leave my father, Domenic and Philo, the only family I've ever had?"

"You'll have to leave your father," Timon said. "You'll have to leave the tyrant who's imprisoned us, the maniac who threatens to kill Lukas if we don't go along with his plans for us and Rome. You'll have to leave Domenic and Philo, too. They obviously knew what your father had in mind for us, and they never gave us any warning. They're the loyal servants every evil king and queen in the world would love to have. They don't question anything he says and does. He saved their lives at the end of the war in Troy, and that's all that matters to them. We don't matter nearly as much. Neither do you."

"We don't give a damn," Lukas said, "whether you consider those people your family or not. You've got to come to Sparta with us. You've got to leave them behind."

"I don't understand," I said. "I'll do everything I can to help you escape Rome. But I don't know why I can't stay here."

I had to admit, though, at least to myself, Timon and Lukas were partly right. I hated the prospect of being separated from them, maybe forever. And I couldn't justify on any ground what my father was doing. His threat to kill Lukas made him a monster, even if he was my father. And Domenic and Philo were going along with him, as they always had. I looked at them when my father made his outrageous threat. They sat on their bench in the courtyard as unresponsive as a couple of lifeless sculptures. But it should've shocked them as much as it did me.

"Think about it," Lukas said. "The only way Timon and I can escape from your father's prison is through this woods and the cave. We'll have to do it at night. We don't want to take any chance at all we'll be spotted between the other end of the cave and the coast where Thalia's ship will be waiting for us. Anybody who sees us will likely alert your father's warriors immediately. No, we'll have to go during the night. When dawn breaks the next morning, we'll need to be on Thalia's ship. So what happens when your father and Domenic and Philo realize that morning we're missing? They know we sleep in your bed with you every night. So what are you going to tell them? You slept through our sneaking out of your bed and your bedroom? We never said anything to you about getting out of here? And somehow we must've discovered a way to do it on our own—when we spend all our time with you?"

"They'll know," Timon said, "you helped us escape. What's your father going to do then? What if he sends a message to us in Sparta threatening to kill you unless we come back to Rome and go along with his scheme to destroy the republic? What if he forces you to send us a message pleading with us to come back here to save your life?"

I had to admit again, at least to myself, my father might do that. I wasn't as important to him as ruling Rome was.

Timon

In the lingering twilight at the edge of the woods, Lukas and I could see Marco was in tears.

"Timon and I," Lukas said, "want you to come with us anyway. We don't want to leave you here. We've told you before, we've fallen in love with you."

"We fear for your safety too," I said.

"Yes, we do," Lukas said. "If Timon isn't here to play king, why won't your father do what everybody assumes he'll do—declare himself the consul? You'll have to fight in the civil war he starts—side by side with him, as you did in Coriolis. If the plebeians win the war, why won't they execute him for committing treason? And why won't they execute his adult son who conspired with him to destroy their republic?"

Still shedding tears, Marco threw his arms around Lukas and me.

"You're right," he said. "I can't stay here. I'll go with you."

Who Killed Coriolanus?

Timon

When we returned to the house from the woods, Domenic and Philo were waiting for us in the courtyard. They sat on the same bench they'd occupied when Old Marco told us I'd become the king of Rome and abolish the republic.

Philo looked up at Marco. "We need to speak with you."

Marco, Lukas and I sat down on our bench.

"Your father has given us some new rules," Philo said. "The three of you are to report to us every time you leave this house. You'll need to tell us what you're up to. Domenic and I will have to know your whereabouts at all times."

Marco rolled his eyes. "How necessary are these silly rules? You'll be guards in a prison, and we'll be the prisoners you guard."

Domenic shook his head. "If I were you, I'd forego the sarcasm. I'd consider myself damned fortunate to live in such a prison. You couldn't ask for more attractive fellow prisoners to spend your days and nights with."

"And your guards," Philo said, "are kindly. At least, I think they are."

"I agree," Lukas said, "you and Domenic are kindly. But what will happen to all of us at the end of the war? Won't we be slaughtered?"

"What war?" Domenic asked. "What slaughter?"

"The civil war," Lukas replied. "The civil war Brutus and his plebeians begin when they refuse to accept Timon as their king."

Domenic scoffed. "They won't dare begin a war. Our warriors will kill as many of them as it takes to put them back in their places. That will be the only slaughter a civil war will bring us."

I looked at Philo. "Do you agree?"

Philo shrugged. "It depends upon how many plebeians choose to fight. They could easily outnumber our warriors."

"And win the war," Lukas said.

Philo shook his head. "We've been given our orders. We can

only do what we've been told to do."

"Even if," Lukas asked, "the orders mean you and Domenic need to spy on Marco, Timon and me?"

Philo shrugged again. "Even if we have to spy on you—if that's what you wish to call it."

Chapter Nineteen

Marco

The next morning my father rose from his bed well before anybody else in the house did. He'd told Domenic and Philo the night before he'd ride his chariot to the army base to oversee the work his warriors needed to do to reinforce the guard posts.

Timon, Lukas and I got ourselves out of our bed earlier than we otherwise would've. We soon saw what we wanted to see—Thalia driving her two-horse wagon toward the house. We went out to meet her.

She told us she'd started out from Ostia as soon as her ship had docked. She'd brought some items from Greece Domenic and Philo had ordered from her. Livia's guards had handwaved her through their post as they always did.

"I can't believe," Timon said, "you sailed to Greece and back in seven days."

"I didn't," Thalia said. "That's the advantage of having two ships. I sailed down the coast of Italy and met my partner in a port we do a lot of business in. We exchanged our goods from Rome and Greece there."

We helped her carry into the pantry the items she'd brought. When we were done, we told Domenic and Philo we'd ride with Thalia in her wagon as far as Livia's guard post and run back home in our loincloths in time to eat lunch with them.

But we never intended to go to the guard post. After we were certain we could no longer be seen from the house, Thalia drove her wagon into a wooded area. As her horses munched on the grass, she stepped down from the driver's seat and sat with us in the wagon bed.

We described for her my father's plan to rule Rome with a captive Timon as a figurehead king.

As she listened to us, she shook her head, sometimes with her eyes closed. After we finished, she went straight to the point. "He'll start a horrible civil war."

I looked at Timon and Lukas. We'd set out in Thalia's wagon already down to our loincloths to make Domenic and Philo believe our story about running home from the guard post.

I knew then I had to do everything I could to free my Spartan companions from the trap my father had caught them in—and had tricked me into helping him do it.

Timon

"So let's consider what you plan to do," Thalia said to the three nearly naked, frightened men sitting with her in her wagon, each of them less than a year past his boyhood. "Let's go over it step by step."

"Marco found a cave," Lukas said. "There's an entrance to it in the woods west of the house. Nobody else seems to know anything about it. He took us through it. There's another opening to it well to the west of the woods and the nearest guard posts. We're going to make our escape through the cave. And we've decided we've got to do it after the sun goes down. We don't want anybody to see us between the cave and wherever we meet your ship along the coast. We think the night will be our best bet for that."

Thalia nodded. "I agree. My sailors and I can pick you up wherever you want. Do you have a particular spot in mind?"

"There's a little cove a bit south of Ostia," Marco replied. "The country in that area is too rough and rocky for raising anything but sheep and goats. But I doubt any livestock or shepherds will be out there in the middle of the night."

Thalia nodded again. "I know the cove you're talking about. We can meet you there in our paddling boat."

"Good," I said. "We'd like to make our escape tomorrow night. The next day I'm supposed to claim my right to be the king of Rome. I want to be gone before that can happen."

Thalia nodded. "You should be gone before that can happen."

"Tomorrow night, though," I said, "the moon will set before we get to the cove. There won't be any moonlight for you to find us."

Thalia chuckled. "We're all seasoned sailors, you know. Starlight will be more than adequate for us. Even if the sky is clouded over from horizon to horizon, we'll find you."

"But we're wondering," I said, "if tomorrow night will pose another problem for you. Will it give you and your sailors enough time to unload and reload your ship?"

"Tomorrow night," Thalia replied, "will give us enough time to unload the ship. But I don't want to reload it before we leave for Greece anyway."

"Why not?" Marco asked. "You surely don't want to go back to Greece empty."

"I want my ship empty when we leave here," Thalia said. "I might need to outrun your father's warships. If I have my ship loaded, I'll never do it. He's got some of the best fighting ships the Greek shipbuilders have put together. I sold him several of them myself. I know the speed they can achieve if they're in the right hands."

"You expect a chase?" Lukas asked.

"I don't expect one," Thalia replied, "but we damned well want to be prepared for one. You're being held here against your will for a reason. You rightly call what you plan to do an escape. The commander of the Roman army and navy doesn't want to let you get away from here. I know him. He'll do whatever it takes to stop you."

"But won't you lose money," I asked, "if you go back to Greece empty?"

"I won't go back empty," Thalia said. "After we're far enough south of here to be out of danger from the Roman navy, we can stop at a port or two and load the ship again. Rome doesn't have that much of interest to me right now anyway. It's a seasonal thing. That's what the shipping business is all about. So get rid of any guilt you might feel over my empty ship. I intend to take you back to Sparta. I want to see the looks on the faces of Helen and the others in your family when they spot you and your friends on the foredeck as we sail into the harbor."

Marco

Thalia turned to me. "We need to focus on ruling out a chase. Even with an empty ship, I could lose a chase to your father's navy."

The three Spartans who sat in a wagon in a woods in the Roman countryside with me were headed to the heart of the matter as surely as the last arrow Timon's father fired at Achilles.

"So what happens," Thalia asked, "the morning after the three of you make your escape and, hopefully, you're on my ship?"

I wasn't ready to respond to that question.

Lukas took it upon himself to do so. "As soon as Domenic and Philo get out of their bed, one of them will come to our room and find out we're gone. They're required to know where we are every moment of the day. They'll have to tell Old Marco we're missing."

Thalia refused to take her eyes off me. "Is that what Domenic and Philo will do?"

"Yes," I replied. "They'll do that. They're loyal servants."

"What will your father do then?" Thalia asked.

This time Timon chose to respond for me, almost as if he and Lukas and Thalia had rehearsed their lines.

"He won't wait a moment," Timon said. "He'll run to his horse and chariot. He'll ride as fast as his horse can take him to Livia's guard post. He'll tell the warriors on duty there they've let his son and the prince of Troy and his companion go missing. By then he'll be certain we're on Thalia's ship. The warriors will race one another to Ostia to see who can claim to have alerted the navy first."

"We can't let that happen," Thalia said, grasping my bare shoulder and shaking me.

"No, we can't," I said—even as I'd already figured out we had only one way not to let that happen.

112

Who Killed Coriolanus?

Marco

Thalia wasn't done with me. "Now we need to focus," she said, "on Domenic and Philo."

I closed my eyes and took a deep breath.

"If you, Timon and Lukas," she continued, "eliminate your father, run to the woods and disappear in it, what will Domenic and Philo do?"

I thought for only a moment. "They'll ride my father's chariot to Livia's guard post. They'll tell the warriors what we've done."

"Is there any way around that?" Thalia asked. "Could you ask them to give you, Timon and Lukas enough time—two or three days, say—to make your escape?"

"They'd never do that," I said. "They'd know they'd be as guilty as I was. When the warriors found out we'd murdered my father, they'd kill Domenic and Philo, probably without a trial."

Thalia nodded. "What if you made Domenic and Philo an offer to take them to Greece with you?"

I shook my head again. "Accepting that offer would be the last thing they'd do. Before Timon and Lukas came along, you were the only Greek they put up with. If my father hadn't saved their lives at the end of the war, the Greeks would've killed them. Domenic and Philo didn't even want my father to invite Timon and Lukas to Rome. Timon was half-Greek, even if he was Paris's son. Lukas was all Greek."

I glanced at the two Spartan men I'd fallen in love with.

"Timon and Lukas can be glad," I said, "Domenic and Phil found them attractive the moment they met them—exceptionally so, they told me. That softened their attitudes toward them even if they were Greek."

"So, no matter what you offered them," Thalia asked, "Domenic and Philo would ride your father's chariot to Livia's guard post and tell the warriors you, Timon and Lukas killed your father and fled?"

I nodded. "I don't have any doubt that's what they'd do. They wouldn't hesitate."

"And the warriors would begin to search for you, Timon and Lukas?"

"Without question."

"What about the navy?"

"Livia would alert them as soon as she could. She knows your ship is here. She must've seen you at the guard post."

Thalia nodded. "She saw me. Do you agree your father's navy would come after my ship?"

"I'm sure they would."

Thalia grasped my shoulder and shook me again.

"We can't let that happen," she said.

"No," I said, "we can't."

But I lost my struggle to hold back my tears.

"You're asking me," I said, as best I could, "to participate in the murders of my father and the two men who raised me, the three people who've been the only family I've ever had."

Lukas embraced me. So did Timon.

"We don't have any other choice," Timon said. "But we know this is awful for you."

"We damned well know that," Lukas said.

No matter how awful it was for me, though, I had to do it to save the lives of the two men who had their arms around me. Timon was right. They and I had no other choice.

Chapter Twenty

Timon

As Marco wiped away his tears, Thalia turned to me. "We need to think about how much time we'll have before somebody discovers what you've done."

"We'll probably have several days," I said. "Maybe even more. The commander of the Roman army and navy doesn't adhere to any schedule. That's for his underlings but not for him. He comes and goes as he pleases. If he doesn't appear at the army base or ships for a number of days, nobody begins a search for him. Nobody pays a visit to his house to see if he's there."

"That's right," Marco said, turning to Thalia. "You're the only person who shows up at the house without an invitation."

Thalia nodded. "That's what Domenic and Philo tell me."

"My father wanted to create an island," Marco said, "strictly for himself, his son and his two faithful servants. Surrounded by guard posts and without unwanted intrusions by other people, they could live on it and tell themselves all was well in the world. I can see that now."

Marco glanced at Lukas and me as if he were confessing.

"Then," he continued, "my father heard the story of the sole surviving member of the Trojan royal family. An idea grew in his mind like a tumor. He decided to invite the prince and his companion to visit his island. He chose not to let them know they'd live on it permanently."

Lukas, who still had an arm around Marco's shoulders, frowned. "That's reason enough, I'd say, to do what we're going to do."

Thalia turned to Marco. "You think your dead father, Domenic and Philo might lie for days before anybody discovers them?"

"I do," Marco said, his tears coming down again. "Our house will smell of death as bad as Coriolis did when we buried the bodies after the battle."

Ron Fritsch

Timon

We interrupted our conversation to view Thalia's stallion mount her mare.

"Are you hoping for a colt?" Lukas asked Thalia.

She nodded. "Assuming I see them again."

"I have a question," Marco said, looking at Lukas and me.

The stallion and mare having finished what they felt they needed to do, Lukas and I turned to Marco.

"How do you propose," he asked, "we kill my father, Domenic and Philo? Do we overpower them individually, and one of us strangles them while the other two hold them down? Or do we suffocate them with pillows? My father will be the toughest of them to deal with, but I'd bet the three of us can do it."

Lukas shook his head. "We've got a less violent plan in mind. We'll tell your father, Domenic and Philo we want to celebrate during our supper tomorrow evening."

"What on earth will we celebrate?" Marco asked.

I laughed. "My becoming the king of Rome the following day."

Marco laughed. "That's a good idea. They'll like celebrating the fall of the republic. They'll be glad to know we want to celebrate it ourselves. But how will a celebration lead to their deaths?'

"Thalia," I said, "brought us something to celebrate with. It's the sweet Spartan wine your father and Domenic and Philo, like the Spartan royal family, are so fond of. It's awfully hard to find this time of the year, but Thalia brought two carafes with her on this trip knowing how much they like it. Lukas and I hid them in the bedroom where we've kept our clothes and other personal belongings during our visit."

"Why did you hide them?" Marco asked.

Thalia and Lukas grimaced in unison.

"Each of the carafes," I replied, "contains enough wine to fill three of our cups. One of us can pour out the contents of one carafe into your father's, Domenic's and Philo's cups. Having emptied that carafe, whoever does the pouring can empty the other one in our cups."

"I'll do the pouring," Marco said. "I assume the carafe intended for my father's, Domenic's and Philo's cups contains poison in addition to the sweet wine they love."

"It does," Lukas said, "but they won't be able to taste it."

"How do you know that?" Marco asked.

"My grandmother Leda told me," I replied. "She put the poison in the wine. You know the story. In her youth she lived in an abandoned house in a royal forest. That's where she gave birth to my mother and my aunt, Clytemnestra."

Marco nodded. "Your grandmother told me that herself."

"She learned a lot of things," I said, "from the vagabonds who passed through the forest from time to time. They showed her which mushrooms were edible and which were poisonous. They also taught her how to make a tasteless poison you could add to a person's drink."

Marco seemed surprised. "Why did your grandmother need to know that? Did she find it necessary to murder somebody?"

I shook my head. "The poison has a beneficial use. That's why she keeps some of it on hand at all times. If persons, usually older persons, become ill and can't find any remedy to relieve their pain and suffering, they send for my grandmother. She goes to see them. If she agrees they're likely to die anyway, but only after more suffering, she puts some of her poison in whatever they want to drink it with. Menelaus and my mother issued a royal decree many years ago authorizing her to do what she does."

"Most of the Greek kingdoms," Thalia said, "have at least one person who can do that."

"Is Leda's poison painless?" Marco asked.

"Painless, yes," Lukas replied. "But at the end, she says, the persons who take the poison know they're dying. They can feel their hearts skipping beats."

"So my father, Domenic and Philo," Marco asked, "will know they're dying?"

"They'll know," Lukas said.

"Will they be able to lash out?" Marco asked. "Will they become violent?"

"No," Lukas replied. "They'll be paralytic by then. They'll be moments away from death."

Marco was wiping his eyes again. Lukas had an arm around his shoulders again.

"I never wanted," Marco said, "your visit to Rome to come to such a horrible end."

Lukas wrapped his other arm around Marco and let him cry on his bare shoulder.

"You'll save a lot of lives," Thalia said. "I asked Brutus what he'll do if your father attempts to abolish the republic. Brutus told me the plebeians loyal to him will fight your father to the bitter end. They're already training for it. Brutus says they'll pick off the warriors individually or in small groups. Then they'll run back to their concealed comrades, enjoy their gratitude and wait their turn to do it again. It won't be an ordinary war like the one at Troy, the one I fought in."

"You fought at Troy?" Marco asked.

Thalia nodded. "I fought your father the day Timon's father died. Your father remembers. Our fighting ended abruptly, though. Moments after cheering the death of Achilles, the Trojan army, hearing Paris had also died, broke and ran."

Marco

After we finished stitching together the threads of what the four of us later referred to as our wagon plot, Timon, Lukas and I ran back to my father's house. We wanted Domenic and Philo to think we'd run all the way from Livia's guard post.

During the run, though, I felt as if I had heavy bags of grain slung over my shoulders. I'd agreed to murder my father, Domenic and Philo. Feeling I had no other choice didn't relieve me of my burden. I was to obliterate the lives of the three individuals I'd lived my entire life with.

After lunch with two of my prospective victims, Domenic and Philo, I complied with the rule my father had laid down. I told them Timon, Lukas and I would be in or near the house all afternoon. If they couldn't see us, we'd be in the woods looking for mushrooms.

When we reached the entrance to the cave, we removed all our clothes. We went to the low part leading to the far western opening, got down on our hands and knees and dug in the earth again. But this time we used the trowels we'd brought from the shed Domenic kept his gardening equipment in. We didn't want to struggle through the cave the following night. We'd have bulging knapsacks with us then.

When we finished our work and returned to the opening to the cave in the woods, we remained naked and carried our clothes to the pond. We needed to go swimming to remove the cave dirt that clung to us like guilt.

After our bodies were clean again, we lay on our backs in shallow water near the edge of the pond. Having agreed to commit three murders, we had nothing further to say.

A young male duck flew down and landed in the middle of the pond, paying no attention to us. Lukas took several deep breaths and slid into the water with the stealth of a snake. As if he were making no effort at all, he swam underwater until he was directly beneath the fowl. Then he rose like an arrow and soon had his left hand clasped around the bird's legs and his right arm wrapped around its wings.

Timon and I found a vine clinging to a tree. We used our trowels to hack a length of it free. When Lukas stepped ashore with his prey, Timon and I bound it with the vine.

The three of us dried off our bodies in the sunlight and breeze in a nearby clearing, put on our clothes and carried the duck to the house.

Marco

"This bird is still alive," Domenic said as soon as he saw it in

119

my arms.

"Which means," I said, "you can roast it for supper tomorrow."

In the warmth of spring in Rome a dead bird wouldn't last long enough for the next day's evening meal. Lukas knew that when he'd set out to capture it alive.

"I promise you," Philo said, "Old Marco won't find any reason to miss supper tomorrow, not if we tell him we'll have roast duck and his favorite wine to go with it."

Timon

Marco and I were damned glad Lukas had caught the duck. Philo's remarks had confirmed our happiness was justified.

Waiting for supper later that afternoon—Domenic and Philo had told us they needed no assistance—we drank plebeian beer on the balcony.

"The next time we can," Marco said, having extended his hand under Lukas's tunic, "you'll find out how much Timon and I appreciate the show you put on for us in the pond."

Marco and I knew how we'd do it. Lukas, who read everything he could find on geometry, called it our equilateral triangle.

Beery plans for future fun and games, though, couldn't conceal how frightened we were.

What if Marco's father, contrary to our hopes, didn't come home for the following day's celebration supper? Did we pour the tainted wine for Domenic and Philo anyway? When, later, Marco's father showed up and asked where they were, did we attack him with a pillow? Even if we eventually accomplished our goal and killed him, could he put up such fierce resistance he'd leave one, two or all three of us with serious injuries, impeding or even rendering impossible our escape?

Those worries and more trailed one after the other in our thoughts like hungry ants slouching towards a pot of spilled honey.

Chapter Twenty-One

Marco

At the supper table that evening I asked my father if the guard posts around the house were fully reinforced.

"No," my father replied, "but they will be by this time tomorrow."

"So you'll be here," Domenic asked, "for our celebration supper?"

My father laughed. "I wouldn't miss your celebration supper."

"You'll be glad to know," Domenic said, "Lukas brought home a live duck he caught on the pond this afternoon. We'll roast it tomorrow."

My father turned to Lukas. "You caught a live duck?"

"You should've seen him do it," I said. "He swam up from below the bird and completely surprised it."

My father continued looking at Lukas as if he were a son who'd accomplished a feat making his father proud. "Thank you. I'll especially enjoy eating your duck."

"You're welcome," Lukas said. "I thought it was the least I could do for the occasion."

Despite the cordial supper-table talk, my father hadn't yet rescinded his threat to kill Lukas if Timon refused to go along with his plan to destroy the Roman republic.

Timon turned to my father. "How do you intend to let the people know I'm claiming to be their king?"

"The morning of the day after tomorrow," my father replied, "I'll go up to the city. I'll stand on the steps of the Curia and wait for the usual crowd to gather. When a sufficient number of Brutus's supporters are present—or, better yet, Brutus himself—I'll state your claim. And, I'll add, the Roman army and navy fully support you. Henceforth, the people will only look to you for guidance on what the laws of this kingdom require them to do or not do. The persons who call themselves senators will no longer exercise any of your powers. The position of consul of Rome will no longer exist."

"Will you go to the city alone?" Timon asked.

My father shook his head. "Not for this. Several dozen of my warriors will accompany me. They'll stand on the steps of the Curia with me."

"Will they know what you plan to do?" Timon asked.

"No," my father replied. "They won't even know they're going to the city with me until I arrive at the base that morning and call out their names. They won't know you're claiming your right to be the king of Rome until they hear me announce it on the steps of the Curia."

"Will I need to be with you?" Timon asked.

"Absolutely not," my father said. "I'd never take that chance. One well-aimed arrow from a rooftop would eliminate the only person in the world who can claim to be the king Rome so badly needs."

"Do any other people than ourselves," Timon asked, "know what you plan to do?"

My father shook his head again. "I first have to make you as safe here as I can. Nobody else will need to know about this until I stand on the steps of the Curia and let the world know."

"What will you do," Philo asked, "if the senators pledged to vote for Brutus defy you and Timon and meet in the Curia the following day?"

"I plan to return to the city with my warriors," my father said. "I'll order them to arrest the so-called senators. I'll never let those traitors take a vote to elect Brutus the consul of Rome."

"What will you do with them?" Timon asked.

"My warriors," my father said, "will try them for treason, find them guilty and execute them."

"Don't you think," Philo asked, "that will start the war Brutus and his supporters want?"

My father laughed. "I'm certain it will start the war I want."

Who Killed Coriolanus?

Lukas laid down the knife he was eating with, placed his arm around my shoulders and turned to my father. "Will Marco need to fight in the war?"

"No," my father replied. "I've considered the matter. He'll do no fighting in this war. I'll appoint him the personal guard of the king and yourself. He'll do so under my order to keep both of you within his sight at all times. If that means the three of you have to sleep in the same bed, so be it."

Lukas looked at me and laughed. "We'll do it for the kingdom of Rome."

Timon

Marco, Lukas and I went to bed that evening as soon as we'd finished helping Domenic and Philo wash and dry the supper dishes.

We chose to spend most of the morning and afternoon of the next day—which we hoped would be our last in Rome—running, working out and swimming in the pond in the woods. After we'd accomplished all that, we sat on a fallen limb we'd pulled into the clearing, letting the sun and the breeze dry off our bodies again.

I looked at Marco. "Your father wants to buy our cooperation. He'd like us to think he's giving us a damned good deal. We'd sit out his war in his modest but comfortable house in the country. We'd spend every day the way we've spent this one, doing whatever pleased us the most at the moment, fed our meals by his servants and protected from the killing by his warriors. All the other Romans, plebeians as well as patricians, would suffer in the war, some of them horribly. If Old Marco won, the surviving people of Rome, patricians as well as plebeians, would hate us. And if Brutus and the plebeians won, they'd execute us as soon as they got their hands on us."

Marco nodded. "That's what would happen to us. We'd be despised in Rome for the rest of our lives, or we'd be killed. I agree with you. We need to crawl through that cave tonight, climb aboard Thalia's ship before dawn tomorrow and leave Rome for good."

Marco

My father suggested we begin drinking the wine in the courtyard before supper. We sat on the benches arranged in a triangle again, all of us seated where we were two days previously when my father disclosed his plan for Timon to become the king of Rome.

I couldn't perceive any difference in the appearances of the two decanters. One stopper, though, was slightly dented. I served that carafe to my father, Domenic and Philo. Thalia had promised us it would be empty at that point, and it was.

I served the other carafe to Timon, Lukas and myself.

"I'm so glad," my father said, looking at the bench where I sat with Timon and Lukas on either side of me, "you three young men have found no reason to oppose my plan to rid our beloved Rome of its damned republic."

Domenic held up his cup as if he were toasting us. "They've made a wise decision."

"Extremely wise," Philo said.

"Eventually," my father said, "I hope to involve all three of you in the major decisions the government of this kingdom requires. I'll train you to take over from me in all matters in my old age and after I die. I want to be known in history as the person who cleverly, adroitly saved Rome as it reached the brink of ruination with a plebeian demagogue as its consul."

"I have no doubt," Timon said, "that's precisely how you'll be remembered in the history of Rome. You'll be praised for what you've done until the end of eternity."

Domenic turned to my father, again with his cup raised. "In our many years of loyally serving you, this is an exciting time for Philo and me. To see you vanquish your enemies so thoroughly has to be the penultimate moment for us."

Who Killed Coriolanus?

Philo also had his cup raised in my father's direction. "You saved our lives during those horrible days when we all thought our monarchy had died. And now you've brought us to its rebirth, to a bright, promising spring after a long republican winter."

That day was cloudless. The air in the courtyard was neither too warm nor too cool. In every direction I looked, Domenic's flowers were in full bloom. None of us seemed able to get enough of the wine Thalia had brought from Sparta as if she were a goddess in an old story.

Marco

My father appeared to be the first to feel the effects of Leda's poison. He set his almost empty cup down on the bench beside him. He touched his hand to the upper left side of his chest. He could feel his heart skipping beats.

Domenic and Philo also set their cups, nearly as empty as my father's, on their bench and touched their hands to their chests.

They and my father saw they were equally afflicted. They looked at Timon, Lukas and me and realized we weren't.

My father attempted to rise to his feet but couldn't.

He saw Domenic and Philo likewise attempt to rise from their bench but fail.

My father turned to me. "You've poisoned us. Our carafe had poison in it. Yours didn't."

"Poisoned," Domenic gasped, looking at me as if I were a stranger and not the loving boy he'd raised. "You've poisoned us."

I had to turn away from Philo. He'd begun weeping.

"Who gave you the poison?" my father asked, his voice rasping. "Brutus? Are you working for him?"

"We got the poison," Timon said, "from my grandmother. We're not working for Brutus. We're working for ourselves. We want nothing to do with the war you want. Your plan to destroy the republic will fail absolutely. Brutus will become consul, for better or for worse. But don't worry. You'll be remembered in the centuries to come. The writers of tragedy will love you. You've swaggered about on your stage as the supreme commander of the hopelessly obedient Roman army and navy, and you've achieved nothing. You've wasted your life."

Timon, Lukas and I could see our poisoning victims were about to fall off their benches. Lukas got up from ours, went to Domenic and Philo and steadied them both. Timon and I went to my father. I took his hands, Timon took his feet, and we laid him on the ground. We laid Domenic and Philo on the ground in the same manner. We didn't want them bruised.

By then, none of them was breathing. None of them had a pulse.

Marco

We went to the kitchen and filled our bowls with the roast duck and greens and other spring vegetables Domenic and Philo had prepared for our supper. We sat at the table in the dining room, without saying a word, and ate our food and finished drinking our carafe of wine.

After we were done with our supper, we had a number of tasks to accomplish before twilight came and we'd need to leave.

We put away the leftover food. We washed and dried the dishes.

We laid my father, Domenic and Philo in their beds. We wanted whoever found them to assume they'd died in their sleep. All the people in a dwelling sometimes did. Nobody knew why.

We tidied every room in the house. We wanted it to look as if nothing dramatic had taken place before the occupants died.

We knew, if our wagon plot succeeded, the people of Rome would eventually learn we were alive and well in Sparta. The story they'd hear would be a true story. I'd fallen in love with Timon and Lukas and decided, as I might, being an adult, I'd return to Sparta with them on Thalia's ship when they did—to remain with them in that happy land for the rest of my life.

Chapter Twenty-Two

Timon

We were about to enter the woods when Marco turned and looked back at the house.

"I've lived here since I was one year old," he said. "I can't remember living anywhere else."

Lukas and I stood on either side of him and looked back at the house ourselves.

"I can understand," Lukas said, "your attachment to it."

"I'll never see it again," Marco said.

"You don't know that," I said.

"I don't know anything," Marco said, "except heartbreak."

"In this world," Lukas said, "that's all you can hope to know. We all die. Every person we love dies too."

I put my hand on Marco's shoulder and shook him, as Thalia had in the wagon.

"Someday," I said, "we might come back here with you."

Marco looked at me. "It's time to go now."

We turned about again and entered the woods.

Timon

When we were inside the cave far enough to be certain nobody outside it could see the torch we'd brought with us, we lit it. We extinguished it when we reached the passage to the opening at the west end of the cave. Our digging the day before allowed us to move through it with some tedious crouching but no need to get down on our hands and knees and crawl.

When we came out of the cave, we were glad the day was still cloudless after sunset. We'd spent some time on the balcony during recent nights attempting to learn which stars would guide us west to the coast and south to the cove we and Thalia had agreed would be our meeting place.

Marco led the way. He needed to carefully examine the terrain ahead of us as we went. Little of it was level and without gullies and chasms of one depth or another we could tumble into. We didn't dare light the torch and call attention to ourselves.

Marco

I would've guessed we were less than a quarter of the way to the coast when we heard several loud exclamations of *yes* arising from a ravine I was leading Timon and Lukas around. I'd remembered it from my earlier treks between the cave and the seacoast. A fall into it would've at least resulted in a broken bone or two.

We all dropped to our knees. I crawled to the edge of the ravine and peered over it. I couldn't take my eyes off what I saw in the starlight until I came to my senses again, knowing I had no other choice.

I motioned to Timon and Lukas to remain in their current positions. I crawled back to them and led them away from the ravine.

When I thought we were far away enough to stop and have a quiet conversation, I sat down on a boulder with sufficient flat surface to accommodate the three of us sitting hip to hip.

Lukas, as I'd anticipated, conducted most of the interrogation.

"Who was in the ravine?" he asked.

"Two men," I replied. "One of them was a warrior."

"Are they following us?"

"No."

"How can you be sure?"

"For one thing, they had no clothes on."

"How did you know one was a warrior?"

"I recognized him," I said. "Even in the starlight, I could see who he was. He's assigned to the nearest guard post. He's only a year or two older than we are."

128

"Who was the other man?"

"A shepherd," I replied. "He's about the same age as the warrior. He lives with his father and mother in the nearest house. We're still on my father's property, you know. They pay rent to my landlord father."

"What was the noise all about?"

"The warrior and the shepherd had finished doing—with great success, I gathered—what they'd decided they needed to do."

"A patrician warrior," Timon asked, "and a plebeian shepherd?"

I muffled my laughter as best I could. "That's why they came out here to do what they did. The warrior wouldn't dare show up at the army base with a shepherd and take him to his bed. And the shepherd's family's two-room house is far too small for him to entertain his warrior friend in."

Lukas stared at me. "You broke the rule. My mother and father were plebeian shepherds. And you're a patrician warrior. But we slept together in your house."

I again had a bit of a problem not laughing out loud. "Prince Timon of Troy also slept in that bed with us. Happily for me, you're the shepherd who comes with the prince, in more ways than one."

Timon

Lukas and I were surprised Marco had remembered the terrain between the cave and the cove so well. The two lovers in the ravine were the only humans we encountered. The stars indicated we could reach the cove within the period of time Thalia had asked us to be there.

As soon as we had a good view of the sea, though, we could go no farther. We saw Thalia's ship where she'd told us it would be. The trouble was, another ship sat in the water next to it.

We quickly hid ourselves behind a thick bush.

"That's a navy ship," Marco said.

"A navy ship?" Lukas asked. "Are you certain?"

"Absolutely certain," Marco replied. "They're built for speed, not for hauling cargo. Even from this distance, even in the starlight, I can see the difference."

I didn't doubt Marco was right.

"Then we're finished," Lukas said. "If the army and navy already know what we've done, they'll never let us leave Rome. We're as good as dead right now."

"Wait a moment," I said, turning to Marco. "Is it possible things could've happened so fast? We'd have to imagine somebody found your father and Domenic and Philo soon after we left the house. They or somebody else they alerted would've had to ride a chariot to Ostia. One of the ships would've had to sail south to catch up with Thalia's. All that between the time we left the house and now? Is it possible?"

Marco shrugged. "Whoever was involved in that would've had to make split-second decisions. The horse or horses pulling the chariot or chariots would've had to be damned speedy. The rowers on that navy ship would've had to pull their oars as fast as they ever did. I suppose it's possible all that could've happened since we left the house. I don't think it's likely, though."

"Maybe that isn't what happened," Lukas said. "Maybe somebody found out about our plot and tipped off the army or navy."

"Who would that be?" I asked. "Thalia was the only other person who knew what we planned to do. I can't imagine she'd do anything to endanger Queen Helen's son and his companion. I doubt her trading business would amount to anything after news of that got out."

"What about her sailors?" Lukas asked.

I shook my head. "She never would've let them know what we were up to. She couldn't depend upon drunken sailors in a port like Ostia keeping secrets."

Lukas shook his head. "She had to let some of them know they were picking us up at an insignificant cove. Wouldn't they think it was odd they'd have to make a stop for us in the middle of the night at such a strange place?"

Marco shook his head. "She'd only be telling them they were

making a special stop to pick up the son of the commander of the Roman army and navy, Queen Helen's son the prince of Troy and the man they were both in love with. Can't people like us ask to be picked up for a voyage to Greece wherever we please? Maybe we wanted to spend one last night in Rome at the cove entertaining ourselves. The two men in the ravine must've loved the night air on their naked bodies."

I turned to Lukas. "Don't forget, we're the three passengers who made things a little bit easier for them. They got to take turns sitting on their asses doing nothing while we pulled the oars and hoisted the sails for them."

Marco turned to Lukas. "I think they liked the three guys who enjoyed playing sailor with them on their way to Rome. That crew would expect to pick them up at a secluded cove before they took them home to Sparta."

"I think," I said, "we should stay right here and wait to see what happens."

"I don't think," Marco said, "we have any other choice. If we left here, where would we go? What plan would we have?"

Marco

Timon and Lukas sat on the ground behind the bush clinging to one another. They made no attempt to hide their tears from me.

Every time I looked at them I had to struggle not to break into tears myself. Gulled by my father, I'd brought them to Rome to die before they reached their nineteenth birthdays. I couldn't blame them if they felt nothing but contempt for me. Maybe it would be some satisfaction for them to know I'd die with them, also before I turned nineteen.

Timon turned to me, wiping his eyes. "What do you see?"

"Nothing, so far," I said. "I'm watching for the navy ship to send a boat this way, loaded with sailors and warriors to search for us."

"What will we do then?" Lukas asked.

"Maybe," I said, "we can try to find a better hiding place than this—like that ravine. The lovers have to be gone from it by now. Both sides of it are steep walls. Those two must've found some safe way to get down to the bottom and back up to the top again. We should be able to do what they did. There's a lot of dead leaves in it. The lovers were using them for a bed. We can use them to cover ourselves. The searchers will take one look, see nothing but leaves and keep on walking. They won't want to risk breaking their necks to make certain we're not down there."

"Sounds like a good idea," Lukas said.

I couldn't detect any hostility in his or Timon's voice. I could only hope they hadn't been attempting to make me feel good when they'd previously insisted they'd forgiven me for what I'd done.

Timon surveyed the rugged landscape. "I don't doubt we can hide from searchers out here. The trouble is, what will we do after they leave? Thalia's ship will be long gone by then. She and her crew will probably be under arrest."

"We'll have to take it one step at a time," Lukas said. "Let's just try not to get caught and survive the night."

"That's the kind of talk I like to hear," I said.

Timon nodded. "Me too."

Chapter Twenty-Three

Marco

I peeked around the bush again. I'd told Timon and Lukas to get some sleep, but I could tell they hadn't even tried to. Their fear had kept them as wide awake as mine had me.

I assumed at first I was imagining what I saw. The longer I looked, though, the more I became convinced what I saw was real.

"The navy ship is moving," I said.

"This way?" Lukas asked.

"No," I said. "It's headed north."

"Back to the navy base at Ostia?" Timon asked.

"We can only hope," I said.

Timon

After the navy ship was so far away in the darkness of the night we could no longer see it, and we knew nobody on it could see us, Marco began leading Lukas and me to the cove.

When we reached our destination, we could see the small boat heading toward us from Thalia's ship. She was the first paddler at the front of the boat. After it came to rest against the sandy beach, she jumped out and gave each of us a hug.

She whispered the same message to each of us. "We'll talk about the delay when we're on the ship again."

We scrambled onto the boat behind her. We grabbed some spare paddles and went to work.

Timon

After we'd climbed up the rope ladders to the deck, Thalia took us to her room. "I assume," she said, "that navy ship frightened you."

"We feared the worst," Lukas said. "At least I did."

"Why was it here?" I asked.

Thalia laughed. "The visit had nothing to do with you. It turned out I'd departed before the Roman navy commanders had decided what they wanted me to bring back from Greece for them. They sent the ship to give me their order. They called it a nighttime training exercise. Most of the sailors looked as young as you."

Marco laughed. "I bet they had a lot of beer on that ship."

"Did they inquire," I asked, "why you were stopped here?"

Thalia shook her head. "They thanked us for stopping as soon as we saw them. My sailors know by now how important it is to curry the favor of our customers. None of them mentioned we were already stopped when we saw their ship approach us."

"So we had no reason to be scared," Lukas said, as if he wanted back the tears he'd shed.

Thalia nodded. "None at all. Now let's talk about more serious matters. Did the poison work?"

"It worked," Marco replied. "My father, Domenic and Philo are dead. We left them in their beds looking as if they'd died in their sleep."

"Nobody saw us," I said, "making our way from the house to the cove. We know, though, you and we could still be in danger."

Thalia nodded again. "If somebody discovers what you did within the next four or five days, the navy might send a ship after me. Beyond that time period, I'm sure they'll realize they can never catch me before I get to Sparta. They won't likely send a military ship into Grecian waters. But while there's still a chance of a chase, I intend to keep this ship moving day and night—as long as we've got enough moonlight or starlight for us to see what lies ahead. I told my crew I'm in a hurry to get to the next port. I said I want to beat my competitors on some deals I think might be available there."

Thalia paused and embraced Marco, who was sitting next to her on her bed.

"Many people should be grateful," she said, "you did what you did. Your father's war would've taken a lot of lives. It could've destroyed Rome."

Timon

"I'd like to ask you," Marco said to Thalia, "for a favor."

"Of course," she said. "What is it?"

"Could we put the bed from my room," he asked, "in Timon and Lukas's room? We'll only need one room for this voyage."

Thalia looked at Lukas and me and laughed. "You can do that—and anything else along those lines you please."

Marco

We worked and ate with the crew again as if we were full-time sailors. Between sunrise and sunset we and Thalia kept ourselves in the stern as much as we could. We wanted a view of the horizon where we'd first see any Roman navy ship chasing us. We took care, though, not to give the crew any reason to suspect what we were doing.

Day after day, every vessel we sighted in any direction turned out to be harmless. When the crew first caught sight of the port Thalia had chosen to load her ship, they hugged one another and cheered. Their days and nights of strenuous work for a benevolent shipowner—she was paying them extra—had reached their end.

Thalia, Timon, Lukas and I embraced one another and cheered as lustily as the crew had. Our days and nights of fear we'd be caught and sent back to Rome for execution had also reached their end.

Timon

Marco, Lukas and I spent the remainder of that day and the next helping the crew load the ship. The following morning we departed the port. Our next stop would be in Sparta.

135

We'd carried out our wagon plot and escaped Rome. We could rationally justify ending the lives of three human beings. We had no other choice—not if we wished to continue our lives with any self-respect, and without the constant fear we'd lose those lives in the civil war Old Marco had his heart set upon. Still, we were in no mood to celebrate.

Marco sometimes woke Lukas and me during our sleep. We'd hear him sobbing. He'd had to murder the two kindly men who'd cared for him since his infancy. It was true they'd made no effort to oppose Old Marco's threat to kill Lukas if I refused to assist him in his effort to destroy the Roman republic. But what other choice did *they* have?

Lukas and I had seen nothing to make us suspect Old Marco had been any less kindly to Domenic and Philo than Thalia was to her crew—or my mother Queen Helen and my stepfather King Menelaus were to the people who worked for them. Old Marco had given Domenic and Philo the freedom to manage his house and raise his son as they chose. If spending their lives working for him had somehow displeased them, they'd discovered an ingenious way to conceal their displeasure from others.

Marco had done everything necessary to murder Domenic, Philo and his father. He'd served them their fatal cups of wine. Lukas and I had told him he didn't need to help us carry our murder victims to their beds and arrange their lifeless bodies to appear as if they'd died in their sleep. But Marco wouldn't let us do it by ourselves. He had hold of the arms or feet of each of our victims when we carried them from the courtyard to their beds. He helped arrange their heads on their pillows and pull the blankets up and over their shoulders.

Lukas and I had found it difficult to sit in the courtyard for a drinking session with our intended victims, and later to tuck their dead bodies in their beds after eating the supper two of them had prepared for us. We could only try to imagine how much more grueling those tasks must've been for Marco.

When he fully woke up during his nighttime spells and realized Lukas and I were with him, he'd stop his frightful sobbing.

"Please don't ever make me sleep alone again," he'd say.

"We'll never do that," Lukas and I would respond.

Marco, the muscular, fully grown man in our bed, would go back to sleep. He'd traded his family for us. We knew our gratitude to him, like that of Domenic and Philo to his father, would continue as long as we lived.

Timon

Lukas, Marco and I stood in the bow of the ship when we entered the harbor in Sparta.

"You have to be there," Thalia had told us.

"Why is that?" I asked.

Thalia once again looked at me as if I were a difficult child.

"Your mother Helen," she replied, "your stepfather Menelaus, your grandmother Leda and your sister Hermione will be on the docks. They won't know whether you and Lukas have survived your adventure in Rome until they see you on this ship."

As we approached the docks, we could see the Spartan royal family was where they'd promised Thalia they'd be.

And they could see Lukas and I were where Thalia had promised them we'd be. They could also see Marco had returned with us. Lukas and I couldn't wait to tell them he'd come to Sparta to live with us.

Timon

Helen, Menelaus, Theda and Hermione rode in one carriage to the palace, and Thalia, Marco, Lukas and I in another. My family wanted to hear, all of them in one session, what had happened in Rome.

We sat on benches in the palace courtyard. How different, I thought, this courtyard conversation would be from the last one Marco, Lukas and I had participated in.

We told our story in its chronological order, from our voyage to

Rome to our return. We didn't tell my family, though, we'd killed three people or why we'd done it. We only told them we'd left Rome before Old Marco declared himself consul of Rome despite losing the election to Brutus. We'd agreed we didn't want to be there after his civil war began. We made our getaway at night through a cave. If Old Marco's guards had caught us, they would've forced Marco to stay in Rome.

"So you don't know yet," my mother said, "how your story ends."

"I'm sailing back to Rome," Thalia said, "as soon as my crew unloads my ship and loads it again.

"Will you be in any danger there?" Menelaus asked. "Won't Old Marco be angry you helped his son leave Rome with his companions?"

Thalia shook her head. "I can't imagine why I'd be in any danger. I only provided passage on my ship to three persons who wished, for whatever their reasons, to go to Greece. How was I supposed to know his son was leaving Rome permanently with his companions?"

Marco

I began working with Timon and Lukas in their olive grove. Their chamber in the palace became my home. We constructed a bed with an olivewood frame large enough for the three of us to sleep on with room to spare.

I no longer worried I'd wake up alone in the middle of the night, after my father, Domenic and Philo once again appeared in a dream, bitterly condemning me for ending their lives for no better reason than continuing my own with Timon and Lukas.

Feeling the arms of my bedmates around me, opening my eyes and seeing them, I'd realize once again the ghosts in my dream had left out of their accusations one of my reasons for doing what I'd done. I'd wished not only to defend my life and those of the men I'd fallen in love with. I'd also hoped to nip in its bud a pointless and deadly war.

Chapter Twenty-Four

Timon

When Thalia returned from her latest voyage to Rome, my mother had a carriage waiting for her at the harbor. As soon as our seafaring guest arrived at the palace, Marco, Lukas and I walked with her to the pond my grandmother kept for the swans. We arranged four benches in a circle in the shade of an ancient oak tree and sat down. Irises, poppies, lilies of the valley and lilacs were in bloom at the edge of the pond.

We had a great number of questions for her.

Marco went first. "Have they found my father, Domenic and Philo?"

Thalia nodded. "Livia found them. More than ten days had gone by since she'd last seen your father, which was the day the warriors finished reinforcing the guard posts. She couldn't find anybody else who'd seen him more recently than she had. She went to the house alone. She discovered him, Domenic and Philo as you'd left them, in their beds. She told the people she could only assume they'd died in their sleep. She hadn't found any marks or bruises on their bodies. Nor had she come upon any evidence of a struggle or violence. The house was in perfect order, as Domenic and Philo had always kept it."

I asked the next question. "Did Livia say anything about our absence from the house?"

"No," Thalia replied. "I told her you were in Sparta. You were passengers on my ship, I said, the last time I'd left Rome for Greece."

"Did anybody want to know," Marco asked, "why I was in Sparta?"

Thalia shook her head. "I told Livia and everybody else I spoke with you'd fallen in love with Timon and Lukas and had decided to live permanently with them in Sparta. No one seemed at all surprised."

"Did Livia or anybody else inquire," Lukas asked, "if we knew

Marco's father and his servants were dead?"

"No," Thalia said. "I told Livia I'd taken the three of you in my wagon through her guard post the day I delivered goods from Greece to the house, the day we finalized our plans in the wagon. She saw Old Marco that day and the next, which was the last day he was alive. I told her you were lying on the wagon bed hiding under the canvas I use to cover the wagon when it rains. I said I took you to a cove south of Ostia to wait for my ship. We didn't want you seen in Ostia."

"You gave us an alibi," Lukas said."

I nodded. "The only people who could say it was a lie were Old Marco, Domenic and Philo, but they're not saying anything now."

Thalia turned to Marco. "When I go back to Rome, I'll tell everybody how devastated you were when I informed you of the deaths of your father and your two servants, every member of your family."

Timon

"Is Brutus the consul of Rome?" I asked.

Thalia nodded. "He is. And so far, things have gone well for him. I advised him he should let the patricians sell their grain for whatever price they can get. He talked the senators into going along with my proposal. It worked too. The grain prices fell. I'd told him they would. I'd seen the surplus grain stored in patrician barns. I knew their owners would rather have indestructible silver and gold locked in their basements than grain susceptible to vermin, mold and lightning strikes in their barns."

"The grain prices," I said, "also fell for you."

Thalia nodded. "I knew you wouldn't fail to notice that aspect of the arrangement. Don't overlook, though, the prices for Roman grain also fell for the people who buy it in other lands, including Sparta."

Timon

Who Killed Coriolanus?

"Has anybody questioned," Marco asked, "whether Brutus's supporters murdered my father?"

"Of course," Thalia replied. "Brutus told me he was certain none of them had. He was very pleased Livia could find no evidence your father had been murdered. Some of your father's most outspoken supporters in the army and navy openly asked if he'd been murdered. Livia thought to take a number of them to see your father's house just as she'd found it. They had to admit to her they saw no evidence a violent murder had taken place."

"Did anybody wonder," Lukas asked, "if Marco's father and servants had been poisoned?"

"That question also came up," Thalia said. "But how could any potential murderers gain peaceful entry to the house and nonviolently administer the poison? How could anybody circumvent the guard posts surrounding the house? So the consensus in Rome, among the plebeians as well as the patricians, is this—Old Marco and his servants committed suicide. They had empty cups on the tables next to their beds."

Thalia had instructed us to leave the empty cups on the tables next to our victims' beds.

"Both Livia and Brutus," she said, "told me they're certain that's what happened. After all, Old Marco had just lost the election to his plebeian archenemy. In the wake of his loss, his only child had chosen to run off to Sparta with Prince Timon of Troy and his companion. Everybody knew how central young Marco was to the lives of his father and his servants. They'd done everything possible to protect him from the outside world. They were obsessed with his security and welfare."

Marco nodded. "I can understand why people see things that way. Not so long ago, I did myself."

Timon

"Livia told me," Thalia continued, "Domenic and Philo knew how to concoct a tasteless and painless poison."

141

Marco nodded and turned to Lukas and me. "They could easily find the ingredients in the woods. Remember the mushrooms?"

"Livia also informed me," Thalia said, "they'd already done it. They poisoned a dinner guest Old Marco had decided was secretly attempting to bring him down."

Now Marco looked as if he'd been taken to another world. "I don't remember their poisoning a dinner guest."

"You didn't eat your evening meal in the house that day," Thalia said. "You were at Livia's guard post. She and her warriors kept you there playing games with them until they learned other warriors had removed the victim's body from your father's house."

As Lukas so often did, he saw fit to extend an arm around Marco's shoulders and speak with him as softly as a loving parent would a child. "That's how your father and Domenic and Philo protected you from the world you lived in—your father's Rome."

Timon

"Does anybody in Rome," I asked, "know Old Marco wanted me to claim my right to be the king?"

Thalia shook her head. "Nobody in the world except the four of us knows that. Many Romans still believe he would've declared himself the consul of Rome if he hadn't committed suicide. But nobody suspects he wished to rule Rome through you as a figurehead king."

"So," Lukas said, "we had no motive to murder Old Marco and his servants."

"None whatsoever," Thalia agreed.

"Nor did we have," Lukas said, "any opportunity to murder them. They were still alive when we left the house in your wagon on our merry way to Sparta."

"That's right," Thalia agreed again. "Nobody has any reason to suspect the three of you murdered Old Marco and his servants."

Chapter Twenty-Five

Timon

Marco began another line of questioning. "Has Brutus named a successor to my father as the commander of the Roman army and navy?"

"He has," Thalia replied. "He appointed Livia to the position. The senate quickly confirmed her appointment. That's something else the patricians and plebeians agreed on."

Marco

"What about my father's estate?" I asked Thalia.

"You inherited it," Thalia said. "Your father left no will. Livia searched the house. She couldn't find one. Brutus told me you're the owner of your father's estate under Roman law."

"Who manages the estate," I asked, "while I'm in Sparta?"

"I do," Thalia replied. "I'm Sparta's ambassador to Rome. As long as you reside in Sparta, I manage your property in Rome in accordance with your instructions. So far, I've kept all of your father's people in their current positions."

"Thank you for that," I said. "I don't want them suffering."

"They won't suffer," Thalia said. "Your father actually treated his employees and tenants rather well."

I nodded. "He did."

Lukas scoffed. "What about the shepherd you saw in a ravine on our way to the coast, living in a two-room house with his mother and father?"

Thalia gripped Lukas's shoulder with her hand and shook him a bit, the way she had me in the wagon.

"I'll tell you," she said, "about that young shepherd and his mother and father in the hills. They don't take their wool and cheese to the village market. They take them to the big market in Ostia. I've gotten a good amount of precious metals in exchange for them here in Greece."

Lukas gave Thalia a skeptical look. "Marco told us there's just three of them—the young shepherd and his mother and father. And you sell their wool and cheese in Greece?"

Thalia shrugged. "They seem to enjoy their lonely way of life in the hills."

"They can read and write too," I said, "Greek as well as Trojan."

Timon turned to me. "But your father wouldn't let them vote. They're plebeians."

I couldn't help but roll my eyes. "Isn't it obvious now? My father didn't really want to let anybody, patrician or plebeian, vote. He thought his was the only vote the people needed. And he'd tell you the shepherd's family in the hills proved it. No other landowner in Rome had tenants like his. Why, he'd ask, do you suppose that was?"

"And he was also willing to kill people," Timon said, "to become what he thought he should be—the sole ruler of Rome. He murdered the sailors and warriors who died at Coriolis. He forced them into a battle they never needed to fight."

"And he threatened to kill us," Lukas said, "if we didn't go along with his plan to make Timon a figurehead king."

"He would've done it too," Thalia said.

"He would've," I agreed. "He would've murdered his only child to get his way."

Timon nodded. "However capable he was, I think we did Rome a great favor when we murdered him."

Marco

"I shouldn't burden you," I said to Thalia, "with managing my father's estate."

"I'd prefer," Thalia said, "somebody else did it."

"The next time you see Brutus," I said, "please ask him if the republic will manage it. Let him know I want all the profit it produces to pay for food, shelter, clothing and other necessities for the Romans who can't afford them."

Thalia nodded. "I'm quite certain Brutus will agree to that. Most of the profit from your father's estate currently goes to the Roman army and navy. Without that source of silver and gold, the commanders of the army and navy will have to look to the senate and consul for tax money for their upkeep."

"Which is the way," Timon said, "it should be. The people, through their representatives, should decide how large and how well outfitted their army and navy need to be."

"For one thing," I said, "they might decide they no longer need to keep a circle of useless guard posts around my father's house."

"Useless," Lukas said, "now that you're gone. What will you do with the house?"

"I'd hope," I said, turning to Thalia, "Livia and her companion could reside there. The commander of the Roman army and navy should have some special place to live in. Do you think Brutus will agree?"

"I suspect," Thalia said, "Brutus and Livia will both consider that a splendid idea."

Timon

I turned to Thalia. "You appear to have a closer relationship with Livia than I'd thought you had when we were in Rome. And she was one of Old Marco's long-term allies."

Thalia nodded. "Livia and I were opponents in Troy. She was on the rooftops firing arrows at me and my comrades. I was on the ground dueling with her comrades. In Rome she was Old Marco's ally, but she also had no wish to see Romans fighting one another in a horrific war. She needed a way to communicate with Brutus."

"And you provided her that way?" I asked.

Thalia nodded again. "I passed messages back and forth between

145

them. They trusted me. They knew damned well the last thing I wanted was the cessation of trade between Rome and Greece a war would bring. They also knew I had a special interest in protecting the three of you. You're the son of the queen of Sparta. I've been more like a sister to her than your aunt Clytemnestra ever was. And Lukas and Marco are your companions. I needed to get you out of Rome if a war came. I made Livia and Brutus both aware of that."

Marco and Lukas were more surprised by Thalia's response to my question than I was.

"Is it possible," I asked, "Livia and Brutus suspect the four of us might've had more to do with the deaths of Old Marco and his servants than they've been told?"

Thalia shrugged. "I don't know what Brutus and Livia suspect. I can't imagine, though, they'd feel any need to know more about those deaths than they already do. Brutus is the consul of Rome. Livia is the commander of the Roman army and navy. Why would persons in those positions question how they gained them?"

"We could ask what you ask," Lukas said, "another way."

"How?" Thalia inquired.

"Why, we could ask, would the individuals in those positions question the person most responsible for Rome's current peace and prosperity?"

Thalia threw her arms around Lukas and hugged him.

Marco and I looked at one another, both of us struggling to remain upright on the tenuous line between laughter and tears.

www.ingramcontent.com/pod-product-compliance
Lightning Source LLC
Chambersburg PA
CBHW061246170626
46809CB00007B/2866